Kingpin Dreams

Paper Boi Rari

Lock Down Publications & Ca$h
Presents
Kingpin Deams
A Novel by *Paper Boi Rari*

Lock Down Publications

P.O. Box 870494

Mesquite, Tx 75180

Visit our website at www.lockdownpublications.com

Copyright 2020 by Paper Boi Rari
Kingpin Dreams

First Edition January 2020
Printed in the United States of America

Cover design and layout by: **Dynasty's Cover Me**
Book interior design by: **Shawn Walker**
Edited by**: Cassandra Sims**

Stay Connected with Us!

Text **LOCKDOWN** to 22828 to stay up-to-date with new releases, sneak peaks, contests and more…

Submission Guideline

Submit the first three chapters of your completed manuscript to ldpsubmissions@gmail.com, subject line: Your book's title. The manuscript must be in a .doc file and sent as an attachment. Document should be in Times New Roman, double spaced and in size 12 font. Also, provide your synopsis and full contact information. If sending multiple submissions, they must each be in a separate email.

Have a story but no way to send it electronically? You can still submit to LDP/Ca$h Presents. Send in the first three chapters, written or typed, of your completed manuscript to:

LDP: Submissions Dept
Po Box 870494
Mesquite, Tx 75187

*DO NOT send original manuscript. Must be a duplicate. *

Provide your synopsis and a cover letter containing your full contact information.

Thanks for considering LDP and Ca$h Presents.

DEDICATIONS

I dedicate this book to all the thoroughbred criminal minds who understood their lifestyles and took sacrifices at a time when life caused adversities to justify their means. The ones who accepted the consequences, however they were issued, without complaining about the outcome of their decisions, and never helped the Ops.

I also have to dedicate this book to all my haters who didn't grow mentally to understand my worth in life. Well, well, well. . . Look at me now! I still got love for y'all because love don't walk away, people do. Facts.

ACKNOWLEDGEMENTS

Mom, first, this is for you: you never judged me on nothing I chose to do in life, no matter wrong or right, you always gave me positive insight on my current situation, and unconditional love. I love you for that and I'm your biggest fan. Love you.

Next up, my father: who didn't understand my rebelliousness but always tried his best to get me on track to live a legit life. When you thought I would never get it right I always heard you—I just wasn't listening at that moment. I stored everything you told me until I was equipped enough to apply it without error, Old Man. You were right all along—the right way is the only way. Love you, Old Man.

Next up is my beautiful daughter Ariana, my little Lady Bug. My most blessed inspiration to want to do better in life. I need to succeed because of you, babygirl. I need to give you the world and everything your heart desires. Daddy loves you with all my heart, mind, and soul. Never question that no matter what the circumstances are. If me and your mom never speak again, you will *always* be number 1 to me, Daddy's Baby Girl! Real Cap.

My second Mom: my baby who helped me see a lot of the capabilities I didn't realize I had. You held me down no matter what, when no one else understood or even tried to understand. I love you for that, Mom. You are an angel.

They say you save the best for last. So, last but not least, God Almighty. I love you, God: for all the experiences you've let me witness and go through. You woke me up to receive my blessings when I was ready for them. I also thank you for letting me realize the powers You instilled in me. I'm your vessel and I'll always trust in You to guide me through life.

I'll wait on Your answers before I respond to any situation. For that, I love You, Father God.

I also almost forgot a few people: City Boi Freak, Chicho D, Blu Magic, 9th Ward God, Lil Big Bruh Leroy, Blacc Tony, GA YamaCraw Slimm, and RIP Scottie 2 Hottie, I know you're looking down on me dawg, you're always going to live through me, bruh. I got you I'll keep you in my memories forever.

Shot out to my dawg, Junkie Git: I had to sit that one out bruh, never hold it against me, it's all love on my end.

Shot out to Lil' Bo, you know what it is my nigga. Oh ni, J-Rock Sin City 4ever homes.

Baby Mama, to let you witness who you should've stayed loyal to is the reason my willpower to win in life is so strong. Now I have to 21 Savage you and Ball with you (S.M.H) But hey, life goes on and then it comes to an end. Decisions, decisions . . .

Shot out to Big Bruh Rod, aka Davis Child, free my nigga, man. I miss you homes, life changed and was never the same after the depart. Hopefully, I'm in position when you reach the turf. I should get there 2 years before you so hey, I'm working.

Like I said, my last shot out have to be to the Almighty Man himself, God. I highly appreciate the blessings.

Oh Dad, all the whoopings finally paid off, huh? L.O.L. If you wonder why your name wasn't called, there are two answers: the first one is because you were not the reason for my penmenship of this novel, but this is only the introduction into the Urban world, so please don't hold it against me—just support the struggle and stay tuned, and if you know me, then without a doubt, you already know you're gonna be involved.

Now, for the second and my most valid reason: because when you thought I wasn't hip to you, I was onto you lames from the start. So, it's only fair that I don't fuck wit' chooo.

It's not what they assume you know, it's what you allow them to see. So, you can control how you choose to deal with an individual at hand in order to reap benefits even they may not know they're giving away, because they're also prospering from you. The only difference is you are conscious of what you allow them to gain, and aware they don't appreciate it. Now understand, as of right now I don't consider myself having any fans yet, only family support. So that's why I didn't mention it.

Again, this is just the intro. So, to anyone who purchases the novel, I hope you enjoy the read. I take pride in my work. Shot out to you all. I love you all, NO CAP, I'm gon' keep 'em coming. I'm here to enlighten you all. I'm making this oath to you all now, *I will never let y'all down as long as there is breath in my body.*

Welcome to Hood Dreams that'll reach every angle of the wrong side of life. I'll introduce you and take you inside Criminal Minds where you feel as if you're really on the scene as it takes place, for a lesser price than really being there, if you feel me.

Enough said, now turn the page and pay real close attention, because if you're not from here, GPS won't even help you get where you're trying to go. Enjoy.

Contact me with all feedback. I also accept email info:
LEVI MADDOX 11807-002
USP 1
P.O. BOX 1033
COLEMAN, FL 33521

INTRODUCTION

Levi Maddox, aka Paper Boi Rari, is currently serving a 144-month sentence for bank robbery. Always trying to escape his current reality and sucker-duck most of the clowns he was forced to be around, he had to find an outlet to keep his mind trained on the task which had led him into the dismal crypts he was now in.

His mind would often wonder off and he'd imagine himself outside the concrete jungle, driving the latest car, flying in the latest jet, or living in a mansion he had designed, himself. With a drive for getting ahead and a sense of independence and success, he is determined to rise to the top.

Poverty was what caused his pain, and it had been the driving force behind the situation at hand. Now, he had to get his revenge, and he would serve it on a cold dish. He reversed his negative into a positive and made poverty bow down to give him success from the experiences of street life.

He picked up a pen and began to describe daily situations which were real facts about life, and how things could turn out when you cheated your way to the top. His motivation evolved from all the haters who ever counted him out, the ones who didn't believe in him, and the ones who thought they could outsmart a man like him.

Attributable to the power God instilled in him, his only desire was to take care of his family and to help communities around the world, by sharing his wisdom.

Paper Boi began penning real hood dreams with hopes of giving his readers a vivid picture into places they had never seen but wanted to understand better.

He lives by one motto: *Never plan because it's not your way but God's way, or no way at all.*

This is his story...

Paper Boi Rari

CHAPTER 1

Lil' Maleek woke up and didn't know where he was to save his life.

"Momma. . ." He cried through the house yelling for his mother unable to find her.

"Momma. . .," he called again.

He was extremely hungry. However, after searching through one of the many unfamiliar houses he'd been inside in the neighborhood, by the age of three Lil' Maleek had gotten used to not being able to find her.

"Shoot, I'm hungry," he said out loud,"I'm 'bout to go find me some food." A few seconds later, he exited the house and pulled the door closed behind him as he stepped onto the porch. He looked around to see if anything looked familiar to him, but nothing stood out.

Born in Detroit, Michigan, where the November winter weather is blistering cold, Lil' Maleek stepped off the porch with no shoes or shirt on in search of something to eat.

As he made his way in the freezing temperature, he came across a convenience store and walked straight through the door. Already predetermined on his destination, he strolled to the middle of the store and walked the aisle looking for one of his favorite foods, the Crunch & Munch. He spotted the yellow box and grabbed it without hesitation then moseyed along to the freezer section. There, he grabbed a box of precooked Jimmy Dean Sausage and Biscuit's. This was a habit he had picked up from his mother whenever they would go shopping—she would always grab items off the shelf and begin eating them as they shopped, which wasn't quite stealing due to the fact she never left the store.

The cashier looking from behind the security glass looked down on Lil' Maleek in disgust, as if he had an ant stuck on the tip of his nose or the taste of shit in his mouth. He shook his head while thinking how could a parent be so careless as to let their child wander off out of their sight like this? But hey, this is Detroit and I've seen worst, he thought.

Lil' Maleek looked up and noticed the cashier glaring from behind the glass, while simultaneously judging the distance from where he stood, to the door. He smiled at the man and in a flash, he made a break for it.

"Hey, come here you little bad ass muthafucker!"

That was the last thing Lil' Maleek heard as he dashed for the door and bent the corner.

When he felt as though he was in the clear, he burst the Jimmy Dean's package open and bit into a frozen biscuit. "Spuh, spuh, spuh!" He spit it out and threw the box on the ground then started on the Crunch & Munch.

"Maleek, Maleek. Bring your ass here!"

He looked up and saw his favorite auntie, Shan. After discovering he was missing, Shan had gone out to search for him. She scooped him up in her arms and could tell he was cold from the way his little body shivered. She noticed the box of Crunch & Munch and wondered where he'd gotten them from.

"Maliss, Maliss!" Ayesha called Maleek by his street name, with much attitude. She stormed in the room and stood with her hands on her hips, bringing Maliss out of his day-dream.

"Yeah, what's up bae?" he finally answered.

"I been sittin' here calling you Maleek, and as soon as I hollered Maliss your ass answered. What was you thinking 'bout that was so important you couldn't hear me, huh?"

"Ayesha what the fuck you want? I ain't on all that," he snapped, in an irritated tone.

Ayesha smacked her lips. "Come downstairs and eat breakfast. You know your princess won't eat until you come to the table."

"Aight, I'm on my way, " Maliss said, then smacked Ayesha on the ass as she walked off switching, extra hard.

A song by Money Bagg Yo blared from Maliss' iPhone 8, indicating he had an incoming call:

I'm trending my shirt / my belt
my shoes dis shit come from Fendi

As soon as Ayesha stepped out, Maliss looked at his cellphone to check the time. Since it was 6:20 a.m. he had a sure guess of who could be calling. He pressed the green illuminated telephone handle on the touch screen which allowed him to answer the call.

"What's up wit' it, bro," Maliss said, as soon as he connected the caller.

"Shid, my lifestyle," Hawk replied, amped up on the other end. "You gon' be on point, ain't you?"

"Ain't I always? Just like a sewing machine, never missing a beat, nigga," Maliss shot back.

"Hell, yeah. I been up all night on this one homes, and lil' buddy strapped. I'm talkin' 'bout gwaped up in these streets," Hawk told him.

"I'm already hip, so look, I'm finna go have breakfast with princess Gabbie before I send her off to school and send the queen off to work. Then I'ma meet you at the spot after the work hour."

"Fasho' my nigga. I'll lace you when you fall through and tell fam I said I send my love, nigga."

"Already," Maliss said, then ended the call.

Antonio Gipps was Hawk's government name and Hawk was the name he'd earned by being super observant in the streets. He took pride in his work which meant doing his homework on nigga's, finding out as much about them as he could.

Hawk was Maliss' childhood partna, and because they both respected the code of the streets, they were more like brothers. Out of the two, Maliss was the oldest, and since he had Hawk by two full weeks, it made him feel like he was his big brother. Their bond had been solidified after meeting in a group home back in the day, when the two friends promised one another they'd stay true till death.

When he was six years old, Maliss moved from Detroit to Alabama to live with his dad, Later, in his teens, his place of residency was in Atlanta, where he stayed with his brother from a different mother, Hawk. Hawk and Maliss together caused more chaos throughout the south than a whole clique of Mexicans could in the city of Juárez. Once Maliss became of age he bought houses in Murthatown Montgomery and one in Phoenix City.

Maliss threw his phone on the super king-size bed and slipped his feet in a pair of Gucci house shoes. He made his way down the stairs to have breakfast with his girls, something he tried to do no matter what came up in his life.

Just as he descended the stairs, "Money Make Ya Handsome," by Gucci Mane chimed through the speakers of his cellphone.

"Fuck," Maliss cursed. Realizing he'd left the phone on the bed, he decided to let it go to voicemail.

"The nigga ain't pick up," Chad told Quan as he put the last stack of money in the duffel bag.

***

Chad and Quan idolized Maliss. They were both at the young age of 19 years old and saw Maliss as the only role model they would ever need. To them he was God himself.

Chad was business-minded with leadership skills, and Quan, on the other hand, was blessed with the gift of gab, his talk-game was his best asset.

The two had been grindin' for Maliss for the past two years—true hustlers who could sell clouds to the sky and grass to the dirt. Them boys had the trap jumpin' for real, selling everything from Legal to Perks.

"Man, we runnin' through bags of this shit fast, ain't we nigga," Chad stated. "When the boss man come through we gon' have to tell 'im to tighten up so we don't have to keep hittin' 'im up every other day."

"Matter-of-fact, text that nigga and tell him the spaceship need gas," Quan said, referring to the synthetic marijuana which they were almost out of.

Designer drug's had taken over the streets, Spaceship, K2, and Ooh Wee were just a few of the names Legal had in the streets, nobody knew what it could be called next.

Chad and Quan were running through one thousand five hundred fifteen-gram packs every two days at $30 a pop. They kept seventy-five hundred apiece and gave Maliss thirty-cents from each one. It made perfect sense since Maliss was the one who funded everything—he had even given them work on consignment.

They contributed 3% of their pay towards the bills in order to keep the trap functioning properly. Since Maliss provided the security in the form of bullet proof vests and heavy artillery, that part of the contract that was nonnegotiable.

"What's the count?" Quan asked as he was checking his IG page.

"Umm, fifty-two cents after our cut," Chad answered.

"Hell, yeah, boy! This shit sweet, bro. That brought us up my nigga, and we ain't gotta put nothin' back in. How can we lose? Plus, I done saved a nice cushion, homes."

"Me too, bro. Big homie good peeps and it's finna get extra gravy once he come on wit' that Molly and Ice Cream everybody screaming about." Chad imagined all the money they'd be making and smiled.

The two MDMA's, also known as Molly, were in popular demand since the streets were gravitating more towards uppers than downers, and Quan and Chad were trying to cash in.

"You know what they say," Quan said, "demand and supply."

"Naw, stupid nigga, it's supply and demand," Chad corrected. As they laughed at the humor between them, Chad's phone came to life.

They got blood on that money and I
still count it / They got blood on the money
and I still count it / I can't help the way I
was raised up

"What's up wit' it, partna?" Chad asked when he picked up.

"Same ol' same ol', lil' homie," Maliss answered, "money, investments, and family. So, what you got for me?"

"Shid, addition, multiplication, and fractions, partna. A lil' division never subtraction, know what I'm talking 'bout?"

Maliss laughed out loud. "Fasho' fam, I can definitely feel that. So look, I got your MSG, so l'ma slide through on y'all boys after I eat lunch, you hear me?"

"Yeah, I'm listening. When you come through, I want to go over the blueprint I been puttin' down, that's if you can find time to fit it into your schedule," Chad replied.

"Yeah, have it lined up for me when I get there. I'ma give you three minutes to convince me on what you talkin' 'bout, or it's gon' have to wait."

Maliss was always putting pressure on Chad to get him to use his wits to its fullest potential. He set out to make Chad sharper than he was. He understood rock sharpened iron, and Chad was going to be his lieutenant, most importantly a reflection of himself. To Maliss that meant Chad was going to have to step up in every aspect of the game point-blank-period.

"Aight that's a bet," Chad said, "in a nutshell, partna."

"Aight. One." Maliss hung up the phone and turned the system up in his brand new drop-top Laguna Blue ZR1. The Corvette was laced with adrenaline red guts, sittin' on 24-inch black Forgiatos. He let the top down at the light while he bobbed his head to the rhythm of "Thug Life" by 21 Savage. The lyrics boomed through the speakers:

> *Scrape da corner / buy a roval dope*
> *inside my grand mom sofa / Sunday family*
> *comin' ova I'm thinkin' to myself you*
> *ain't gang nigga fuck you / feel like Tu-*
> *pac thug life nigga fuck you*

Everybody Maliss passed stared at his whip. He had nearly 2000 horses underneath the hood, so the Vette esounded like a monster as it rumbled the ground through the exhaust system.

One day Maliss developed the courage to mash on the gas, and that was a day he'd never forget. *That bitch fishtailed sideways almost four lanes and three blocks in a matter of seconds,* scaring him half to death. He laughed out loud at the thought of it while he admired himself in the rearview mirror sporting a bruhnd-new pair of Yah's.

"Where you at, bro?" Hawk asked, his voice coming through the system unannounced.

"I'm on my way," Maliss responded. "Nigga, get off my line," he half-joked, aggravated that his song had been inter-rupted.

"Damn you, nigga. Hurry up, work need to be done."

Maliss listened to Hawk rant a little bit then ended the call.

CHAPTER 2

"Hi, this is Robin Meldows live on HLM and this is Breaking News: A woman was found dead due to an overdose of Fentanyl. This is the 224th case in our community involving death caused by overdose with traces of the Fentanyl Opioid. As of right now, the deceased woman's name has not been released due to pending investigation. However, authorities do have a suspect in custody by the name of 26-year-old Randy Mills.

Mr. Mills was charged with murder and his bond was set at two-hundred fifty thousand dollars. We will keep you informed as we receive updates on this case.

In more Breaking News: man shot twenty-two times in his grandmother's yard by Sacramento police . Again, just in minutes ago, another tragedy. Police shot and killed a gun-wielding suspect in an attempt to unarm him. We will report back as soon as we have more information on this matter. This is Robin Meldows at HLM News."

lst Degree shook his head and turned the flat screen off as he continued to get head from this lil' groupie bitch named Tina.

"This shit crazy," he said, "all these people dyin' from drugs and these pussy ass crackers killin' our people for bullshit and gettin' away wit' it, and aint nobody standin' up for shit 'round this bitch."

lst Degree was an up and coming popular rapper from Sin City, Alabama, known as Phenix City. He was on his Black Lives Matter tour and the streets were fucking with him tough.

Slurp, slurp, slurp . . . Tina hadn't missed a beat with the hot, slow, deep throat treatment she was serving him.

"Ssss ... Sh-it," he said. "Umm-hmm . . . just like that girl."

Slurp, slurp, slurp . . . She knew she was the shit in the brain department, and she was trying to take his mind off the depressing situations that had just occurred that day.

"Relax, baby," she whispered.

Slurp, slurp, slurp . . .

"Umph, umph, umph. God leeee," 1st Degree said through clench teeth. "Ssss . . . here that . . . shit . . . cum . . . bitch," he managed to get out, as he grabbed the back of her head and pushed himself deeper down her throat. He busted all down in it and never once did Tina gag. She swallowed every drop and drained him completely.

Afterwards, she begin to clean him up, and as she did, she looked in his eyes and sucked the tip of his head a little more. Teasing and licking it a few more times, she tucked his member back in his Tom Ford boxer briefs then picked the money up off the table and got off the tour bus, leaving him to his thoughts.

"I'm finna write a Fuck the Law track, ah Safe Sex track, a Stop the Violence track and a Drugs Kill track." 1st Degree picked up his iPhone and hit up his favorite producer and DJ, DJ DNT Panic.

"Wat's up, bro?" DJ DNT Panic said upon answering.

"Man, I need you to put me some heat together in that kitchen. I'm finna go in for the hood, bro."

1st Degree explained what he wanted and Panic loved his idea. He loved it so much that as soon as the call ended he went straight to work on it.

Since 1st Degree and Panic had already been vibing for a while now, Panic knew how to produce it for him without him being there. Then, he would send the tracks to him when he was finished, and together they would make history with 1st Degree's raspy voice. 1st Dagree would go on to be the voice for the people and the people's champ.

Funny thing though, he was an addict who loved Promethazine known as *kickstand* on the streets because it caused its users to display an exaggerated lean. Plus, he was fucking wit that space, which is synthetic weed.

After he hung up with DJ DNT Panic, he drifted off in a mean heavy nod off the purple syrup and came up with a hit for, Fuck the Law, which would become number one on the Billboard charts in the country, giving him the status of the boldest and hottest rapper alive.

CHAPTER 3

Maliss pulled up at The Spot, a stereo shop he and Hawk owned together. As he walked in, an unfamiliar beat was blasting from the speakers in the shop, "Chance" by Lil Baby & Marlo, off that "2 The Hard Way" track:

All I needed was a chance
all I needed was a chance
all I needed was a chance
watch me run up those bandz

Hawk looked up from the DuPont Registry Homes magazine he was looking at and saw his partner coming his way. He got up and greeted him with love in his eyes.

"Who this nigga?" Maliss asked Hawk.

"This, uh, them lil niggas from Atlanta, um Lil Baby dem.

"That shit fire, right?" Maliss asked in an animated tone.

"Hell yeah, but what's up doe, bro? What you got for me?" asked Hawk.

"Let's go to the office so I can lace you up," Maliss replied.

Once the two were in the private confines of the office, Hawk put him on game with the Mexican who was known to hang out at David's & Buster's after hours for the poker game. The same Mexican, whose name was Carlos, been in the city for about six months now, and they had been shoppin' with him for a month. Carlos was also the one behind the Legal and the Percs that they were fucking with.

"So, this the deal bro . . . I finally got in wit' Universal Spys, and this lil' lame ass nigga who like Percs got me a few trackers that ain't have to be registered, ya feel me?"

"Yeah," Maliss said, listening attentively, "we already know he stay out in Gwinnett, right?"

"We also know he drive a black F350 and also a silver Porsche 911, right?" said Hawk.

"Right," Maliss affirmed.

"I figured next time y'all play poker I could hook up one of the trackers on his whip and the the rest is history, bro," Hawk concluded, sure of himself.

Maliss sat quietly for a minute since he was the actual master mind. He would put the formula together to ensure the plan was executed throughly.

"So," Maliss said, as the wheels of his mind began to turn, "tonight is the poker game, right?"

"Right," Hawk confirmed. Now it was his turn to be attentive.

"We know Dave & Buster's closes at 11:30 p.m., right?

So, at 12:15 a.m. they'll be ready to start the games like always, and you'll need to be in the parking lot by 11:00 p.m., so that gives you a whole hour and some change to scope the scene, you feel me?" Maliss said.

Hawk didn't respond so Maliss took that as his cue to continue.

"I figured Carlos would probably arrive round 11:45 and and 12:00 p.m., right?"

"Yeah, that's right," Hawk agreed.

"So you should get to see anybody who arrives, bro. I'ma pull in at 12 p.m. sharp and go 'head in. And since this wetback be on my sauce so bad, it'll give him the time he needs to glorify me for a few minutes before I take his gambling money, then his life savings, you feel me?" Maliss laughed.

"Once you have the tracker in place, text me. I'll know it's you 'cause we the only ones who got these phone numbers. Besides, these can't be traced or tracked anyway. But now that we got all that out the way, once the tracker is activated, how long we got before it goes out?"

"It least twelve hours," Hawk said.

"Oh, hell yeah, boy, that's great timing. So, with that said, I guess I get to rob myself today," Maliss replied then chuckled.

Hawk laughed too then asked, "What you talkin' 'bout? Like that Plies song, nigga?"

"Hell nah," Maliss replied. "I mean I gotta put my young boys to the test today and see if they ready for the next level I'm. If they pass, they in, if they don't, they get extinguished, you feel me?"

"Yeah, so what the lick read?" Hawk asked.

"Well, I gotta go pick up this lil' change from the trap then I'll restock 'em. Chad said he got a blueprint he made especially for me. I'ma go and give him three minutes to explain it. If it's right, I'ma fuck wit' him, if it's not then they stay where they at until futher notice. Then, we'll double back around, let's say, 7:30 p.m. and hit 'em and see how it goes. As a matter of fact I'ma leave the bread in the safe and use it to my advantage. Feel me, bro?"

"Yeah, that's fire, nigga. How you be comin' up wit' this shit?" Hawk asked as if he were amazed.

"Freestyle," Maliss said. "Freestlye, my nigga."

"Nah, that ain't it, 'cause ain't shit free 'bout the style," Hawk replied. "Niggas gotta pay for the game to play the game, bro."

"Hell yeah, nigga. You already know." Maliss smiled. "So, check it . . . all this shit gotta be precise 'cause you already know I gotta be there when princess Gabbie wake up so I can eat breakfast with her before she go to school."

"Fasho'," Hawk said.

Maliss looked at his Patek Philippe and saw that it was 11:45 a.m.

"Well bro, that's all I got for today homes, what about you?"

"Me too, bro," Hawk said.

"Aight, I'm finna stroll on and put some shit in motion then. One," Maliss said.

"One," Hawk countered. The two stood to their feet, hit each other up with some dap then they headed to the front of the store.

Business was booming and there were six cars getting hooked up with L7 Subwoofers.

"Do that shit!" Maliss said to Hawk as he exited the store.

* * *

Click, Click, Click. The camera flashed as the Feds took pictures of Maliss from across the street as he got inside his ZRl Vette.

"That's him," Agent Malone said to agent Patricia. "That's Maleek Davis right there. Maliss the great, the drug lord king pin." However, Maliss was far from a drug lord, if only he knew.

Maliss sat in his car searching for "Chance" by Lil Baby & Marlo featuring Kollision, before he took off in the super car being followed by the Feds.

On his way to handle business, he decided to take Ayesha some Snow crab's, shrimps and fried rice for lunch before hitting the interstate. The Vette was so fast, he bypassed everything moving.

He came up on Old National on the South side of Atlanta where one of his traps was located.

CHAPTER 4

Sin City was J-Rack's city, well use to be his city. Nowadays everybody was fucking with the duce and not the loud, which meant business was falling off for J-Racks. Duce was another term for the synthetic, legal, K2, spice or spaceship. Dealers could pick any alias they wanted to for it, but at the end of the day, it would still have precedence on the streets.

Cocaine had finally fallen off the map cause ice and Molly had replaced it—J-Racks could barely move five units a month now in Sin City, and he was in rage because it was fucking up his paper.

"Man, I hear them young fuck-niggas on the South Side got the whole city on smash," J-Racks said to his older brother Red Dog, who had just finished a 30 year Fed beef.

"Yeah, I heard of 'em all the way cross the country at Long Pack," Red said.

Lil' Fred and Lil' Rod were the talk of the town, riding Vettes and Camaros, having throwback parties and helping the elderly, while giving to the churches. They were killing anything that got in their way, but little did anyone know, Maliss was the mastermind behind the scene. He had organized the entire structure from out of state, and he was the one responsible for flooding the city with the poison that had the young generation going crazy.

"What's up wit' it, Lil' Rod?" Lil' Fred said, as Lil' Rod walked in one of their spots over in Asbury on the .

"You know what it is," Lil' Rod said, "just comin' from down the road." He dropped the duffle bag on the floor before adding, "Them country boys get money down there. We need to buy some land down there and open up a meat market or somethin', boy. It would be a super advantage for us."

"We'll see, but for now, let's just stack some more bread," Lil' Fred said. "So what's the count 'cause bruh should he comin' through after a while."

"Turn Out the Lights" by Future came through Lil' Rod's iPhone 8 and interrupted before he could answer. "Hold on, bruh," he motioned to Lil' Fred by holding his index finger in the air. What's up, B?"

"Where you at?" Amy asked.

"Where I'm always at, B. What the lick read 'cause I'm busy right now," he said.

"Fuck all that! You always say that same shit," Amy replied with attitude.

"Fuck you talkin' bout'?" Lil' Rod asked.

"You bet not be fuckin' wit' them nasty ass hoes, Rodrick!" she added.

"Man, I'm on this Gwolla Boot, fuck you mean. I ain't know *you* was a nasty hoe. Thank you for the intell."

"Boi, I ain't no hoe. You got me fucked up," Amy said.

"Well you the only one I'm fuckin', so you must be talking about yourself. Don't you do yourself like dat."

"Well, why every time I call you rushin' me off the phone?" she asked.

"'Cause I'm at work, bae, and when you at work you don't mix business with pleasure. Now if you don't mind, I have to get back to work," Lil' Rod replied, hoping to ease Amy's mind.

"Well, I was just callin' to hear your voice. I love you, Rodrick."

"I love you to, wifey." Hearing herself referred to as *wifey* caused Amy to blush, especially since the two weren't legally married yet.

"Well, you fuckin' up Rodrick and you finna be in the doghouse if you don't start spendin' some time wit' me."

"So, I guess them diamonds and shoppin' sprees ain't enough then, Lil' Rod asked.

"No," Amy pouted. "Fuck that shit. I want you, Rodrick, but I 'preciate and like 'em," she made sure to add.

"Okay, bae, I got you. We gon' fuck around."

"Boy, you better stop playin'g wit' me!"

"Aright, Amy. I'ma show you more affection and I'ma work on spendin' more time wit' you, okay, B?"

"Okay, bae. I love you, husband."

"Love you too wifey, now bye."

Click. Lil' Rod hung up.

Vrmm... Vrm...

No sooner than he had, his phone immediately sounded off informing him he had received a text message. He opened it and read it:

Doghouse! It was from Amy with a sad face.

Lil' Rod showed Lil' Fred and both men got a good laugh.

"Now where were we before wifey interrupted us? Oh yeah, the count is 242 bands includin' this duffel bag from the lil' homie," Lil' Rod said

"Aight," Lil' Fred said. "How much inventory we got left?"

"Enough for four more days."

"Let's band the bread up in the duffel bag and secure the bag, then we can get on this Madden 19 one time for a band a game," Lil' Fred said challenging his partna.

* **

Meanwhile at the precinct, Lieutenant Barns and Sergeant Hawkins were investigating Freddie Longs, aka Lil' Fred and Rodrick Miles aka Lil' Rod, on all types of shit. Drugs, murder, extortion and some more shit. They wanted their supplier, but they were having difficulty getting close to them. Now, they were considering turning the case over to the good old boy up in the Capital, up in Murda Town, Montgomery.

"Hey girl," Ayesha said into the phone, talkin' to her best friend, Santanna, who was down in Haynesville, Alabama.

"Ain't shit, girl, finna get ready to go shoppin' for Swolehead's pool party this weekend 'cause that bitch gon' be live, Nicky," Santanna said to her best friend.

Nicky was Ayesha's middle name and the only name Santanna referred to her as, unless she was mad with her.

"Everybody gone be there. Plus, he got the Migos comin' through and I heard that Lil' Wayne is supposed to slide through, too," Santanna informed her friend.

"Lil' Wayne?"

"Un-huh, Lil' Wayne, girl."

"Stop lying, girl 'cause you know I love me some Lil' Wayne, Cormesha," Ayesha said, likewise calling Santanna by her real name.

"Um-hmm, that's what I heard, babygirl. Too bad Maleek got them cuffs on that ass 'cause it would be nice to kick it with you, but you in the big city now so you see celebrities all the time anyway. Besides, you know your little boo thang, Lil' Wee Wee gon' be there," Santanna said teasingly.

"Umm-hmm, look Santanna I'ma work on that with Maleek. Just give me a day or two to come up with somethin' 'cause I got to go to this concert, plus Lil' Wee Wee callin' me now, and I got work to do and money to make." Lil Wee Wee was her side piece from back in the day.

Nicky owned a Tax Preparation business, and because it was the month of May business was slowing up. She was preparing to close the shop until the following tax season and work from her laptop—it was either that or get a side hustle.

After hanging up from her girl, Ayesha answered her boo's call all sexy-like. "Hellooo."

"What's up, Nicky bae?" Lil' Wee Wee said.

"Who the fuck is dis?" she feigned an attitude, fucking with her boo thang's head.

"This Wee Wee. Stop playin' like you ain't got caller ID or somethin' fo' I come up there and beat that ass real quick."

"I'm just messin' wit' you. "But, you know I live with my crazy ass baby daddy, so I try to stay on point."

Lil' Wee Wee to laughed. Bitches were forever creeping, but he wasn't about to judge her. Instead, he said, "Damn, I miss you, Nicky. I need you bad. I miss that super wet pussy, girl."

"I know you do. What? Yo' ol' lady can't keep it up for you?"

"Nah, this ain't about her, this 'bout you. Look, fuck all that, I need my meds, Nicky. Now what's up? You been promised me you was gon' come give me some, so you the one who ain't keep yo' end of the bargain. It look like I'm the one who gon' have to come up there and get it, so give me the directions," he asked seriously.

"Okay, first you get on 85 North, then you go this way and that way." She laughed.

"Stop fuckin' around, Nicky." He was beginning to get an attitude.

He wanted to fuck the shit out of Ayesha and she knew it. She had the best pussy he had ever had in his life, and she was by far the finest bitch he had ever been with.

Ayesha was five feet three inches tall and weighed one hundred thirty-eight pounds with C-cup titties small enough to bite. She had a super phat ass with the prettiest feet plus she was bow-legged as hell.

"Boy, stop being dumb. I don't fuck where I live, are you crazy? I'm livin' like them movie stars. Nigga, I wouldn't fuck that up for Jesus himself, especially since you can't support me like that. But I'm finna try to get away this weekend and slide down the way. If I make it, I'll come put this cupcake in yo' mouth and give you a little taste of my sweetness, okay? I gotta go now though, boo-thang, but don't be callin' this number no more, I'll call you. I told you that before. If you do it again I'ma change my number and we'll be through forever. Now bye!"

Click. Ayesha hit the end call option and put some thought into her plan of getting away to her home town for the weekend without raising Maleek's suspicion. Since everyone on both sides of her family still stayed in Hayneville, she would have a legit excuse to go visit.

"Stupid bitch!" Lil Wee Wee cursed. *I got somethin' for that smart mouth of her's when I catch up wit' her—a hard dick and plenty of cum."* He laughed out loud as he continued *talking to himself. And since she got the big head, I'ma put a dent in that lame ass nigga Maliss' pocket too. Yeah, I got somethin' for her stuck-up ass. Right after I fuck her one more time tho'.* He smirked deviously.

***

"I told your ass nigga, dem sorry ass Falcon's couldn't beat my Denver Broncos, boy!" Lil' Fred said to Lil' Rod, as he threw the wireless controller on the couch and snatched the stack off the coffee table. He had just hit Lil' Rod for three bands playing Madden 19.

"Foxy Lady on you tonight, nigga," Lil' Rod said as he watched Lil' Fred laughing out loud holding a fist full of money in the air. Foxy Lady was a strip club in Columbus, GA, located on Victory Drive, across the bridge from Sin City.

"You want somethin' to drink?" Lil' Fred asked, making his way to the kitchen.

"Yeah, grab me a Bud Lite, bruh, 'preciate it."

"Yeah, I got yo' fuck ass. Took some of your bread bitch-ass nigga, next it's gon' be your life, you and that lame ass nigga, Maliss, since you always dick ridin' 'im. Then I'ma be the one runnin' this shit," Lil' Fred mumbled to himself *This J-Rack's city anyway. He just ain't had time to see the potential in me yet, but after this, he gon' even have to bow down and get on my team.*

He got the Bud Lite from the fridge and turned it upside down. He stuck it in his pants and rubbed it around his dick. *Suck my dick, bitch-ass nigga.* Then he took the bottle and rubbed it on his ass. *And kiss my ass too, fuck-nigga.*

When he finally went back to the living room, Lil' Rod was on the phone with Maliss. Lil' Fred handed him the beer with a smirk on his face. Lil' Rod shook his head and accepted the bottle; however, he had failed to notice the hater-aid Lil' Fred was displaying. If anything, he thought Lil' Fred was still riding the wave from the bread and games he'd won.

"Oh, aight then, big bruh," Lil' Rod said talking to Maliss. "Fasho', yeah, we got you . . . it's a done deal then." He paused momentarily as he listened then continued. "Man, it is what it is. Yeah, we should be good. Okay then, one," he said before pressing the end call on his phone.

"What's up?" Lil' Fred asked.

"That was bruh. He said he gon' be a little late on the delivery tip, but to just be cool 'cause he got somethin' for us."

"Okay, did he say how late?" Lil' Fred asked.

"Nah, he just said be cool he got us."

"Aight then," Lil' Rod nodded.

Boom, Boom, Boom, Boom!

A knock came at the door. Lil' Fred walked over and opened it but made sure to leave the security door with the slot in it, locked.

"What's up wit' it, Lil' Fred?" asked a customer, also referred to as a custo. "Let me get a ten pack," the custo said and slid three-hundred dollars through the slot.

"Aight, hold on a second." Lil' Fred slid the slot closed and went to retrieve the product.

***

J-Racks was across the street waiting for the product so he could go on the other side of town to break it down. He wanted to get a real feel for the clientele before investing any *real* money into it.

"This lil' bitch-ass nigga servin' me for now but watch this," J-Racks said to Red Dog.

"Yeah, don't trip," Red Dog said. "Man, we gon' shut this shit down. I told you my dog finna get out and he said he got that shit by the truck load, lil' bruh. That shit run the system. We got to stick to the old code . . . Out hustle 'em and kill 'em or put them folks on 'em."

"Man fuck all that. I ain't wit' that sucker shit, bruh. As a matter-of-fact, don't let that shit come out yo' mouth 'round me no' mo', home. Fuck you get that from? Talkin' 'bout put the folks on 'em? Fuck outta here," J-Racks said.

Red Dog had worked with the authorities on his first Fed bid and still couldn't get less than thirty years. He kept his mouth closed but he knew he was about to branch off from his little bruh because before he'd gone to prison he had been his own boss. He would be damned if he was going to start taking orders from his younger brother now, especially since he was the one who had given him the game. *Let the chips fall where they may*, he thought.

CHAPTER 5

"It's 1:30 p.m." Quan, a youngster with zero patience said.

"I know, and time is money," Chad said. He stood up and went over to look out the window. He noticed Maliss was right on time as usual. He watched as he put the top back up on his Vette.

"Shit, he said after the lunch hours but he ain't showed up yet. I'm finna text that nigga," Quan told Chad.

"Nah, bruh, fall back . . . He out there right now. You just gotta learn how to have patience. A man in a rush will always forget somethin', fumble the ball, or make someone in his presents fumble, bruh," Chad said, schooling the youngster on the facts of life.

"Yeah, yeah, yeah keep all that conscious shit for a standup play or somethin', nigga. I'm in the left lane wit' one gear and that bitch wide open, homes, you hear me?" Quan responded.

Maliss hit the button for the secret compartment hidden inside his car, and the back of the passenger seat leaned forward and split in the middle.

He pulled out a Ziplock bag with a quarter pound of Perc and another vacuum sealed bag with fifteen hundred packs of Space in it. He also hit them with about two gallons of Kickstand so they would have something to keep the customers coming when they got low on the Space and Percs.

He texted Chad and told him to get the door ready, then he secured the stash spot after grabbing his FN. He looked around to make sure everything in his surroundings was in place before stepping out of his whip.

"Alright here we go," Maliss said to himself.

He got out and tucked his pistol under his left arm pit and held the bags in his left hand, inside a briefcase, then took long strides to the entrance.

***

"Fuck," Agent Malone said, "we lost him again. That muthafucker drives like a Nascar racer or something."

"Umm-hmm," Agent Patricia said, secretly admiring Maleek to herself. "We'll get him, eventually. Everyone has a pattern and he's bound to slip up in a minute. We just need to be there to catch him."

"Hell nah, when he slips, I want that scumbag to fall hard. As a matter-of-fact, I'm trying hard to be the one who pulls the carpet up from underneath him and watch Judge Elks sink his ass with an elbow and hope he gets killed somewhere in the U.S.P," he said, wishing a life sentence in the United States Prison system on Maleek.

***

"So, check it out, man. We done picked up some heavy clientele now, bruh, and we need to up our inventory so we ain't gotta keep callin' you for the reup every two days. In business you have to see growth and that's what we been seein'," Chad said.

When Maliss didn't respond, Chad continued.

"Everybody askin' 'bout that Molly and Ice, so I think we should add that into the invo too, big bruh. We can go over the numbers later and the rest is history, and that's it in a nutshell, partna."

Maliss remained quite for a minute while he calculated the numbers in his head.

"Let me ponder on it some more and I'll get back at y'all boys, but it does sound like a plan I can see myself considering," Maliss said.

"Yeah, and I'm not sayin' the formula you got set in place ain't workin' but we in this to grow, bruh. Everybody is controllin' their part good so far. We been two years runnin' and still no fumbles," Quan said, shaking his head. Malisswas silent but mimicked Quan's head gestures, also shaking his head in the affirmative.

"So, look, this the same setup as usual," Maliss said, putting his briefcase on the table before opening it. He handed the pack to Chad. Quan went in the back to get the bread out of the safe. When hecame back, Maliss was gone.

"Where he go?" Quan asked somewhat confused.

"He said he'll get it later. He didn't wanna travel wit' the bread right now. He said he had an eerie feelin' and he knows he can count on us wit' his money," Chad answered.

"Aight, bet that, " Quan said before going to secure the bag.

At 2:45 p.m., Quan and Chad's phone began jumping like a Verizon telecommunication company. Cars were pulling in and out like it was Friday night at the ABC store. The two were boys were slinging packs back-to-back like Drake making hits.

"Let me get a thirty piece," a custo said.

"Let me get a hundred of them Percs," another said.

"I need a Spaceship wit' a hundred," said another.

"Let me get an eighth of that Kickstand, homes," and just as soon as they filled that order, four more came.

"Shit, nigga it's 5:40 p.m., shop closed, fuck that. Let's do a invo check right fast. I know we just boomed at least half of everything, Quan said, suggesting they do a quick inventory on what was sold and what was made.

"Yeah, you right," Chad agreed.

After they finished with the inventory they discovered they were both right. They had finished half of everything except the Lean and they only had a eighth left of that.

"We might as well split this," Quan suggested.

"Nah, I'm good," Chad said, declining the offer.

"I'ma cover it broke-ass nigga."

"That ain't the issue, homes. I'm just coolin'." Chad was adamant.

"Fuck all that coolin' shit," Quan said. He walked away and headed for the kitchen. Pressure bust pipes, and he wasn't taking no for an answer. Chad was going to sip the Lean today, because that's what they did, simple as that.

Quan grabbed a pineapple Fanta soda out of the icebox. He grabbed four styrofoam cups and doubled them up, making two cups. Then, he put some crushed ice in both cups. Afterwards, he crushed up six percs and sprinkled them on top of the ice, then poured the Lean and the soda down the side of the cup so it wouldn't fizz up, which would leave more room for more of the liquid drink to be added.

Swoosh, swoosh. swoosh . . . He jiggled the cup around to make sure everything was well mixed. "This bitch gon' be like that," Quan said, as he finished mixing the drink.

By the time he'd gotten back in the living room Chad had finished rolling the blunt.

"This that Mango Kush wit' that bling-bling monkey," Chad said, "straight gas, ya' hear me."

"Yeah, fire that shit up then, let's see," Quan told him. Bling-bling monkey was a kind of K2, but it was much stronger compared to what they had been smoking—two hits was like a whole blunt of loud.

"I got them hoe's I met on Tiny Chat.com on the way, bruh."

"Oh yeah," Quan said, starting to feel the effects of the Kickstand.

Chad hit the blunt four times, and because he was so high, he held it in his hand, before passing it to Quan. Then, he grabbed the cup of lean and took a few good sips before setting it back down.

Swww... swww... swwww... "Here, nigga." Quan passed it back to Chad.

"Yo', I'm already high as hell, nigga," Chad said, slurring his words from the effects of the Lean he'd decided to sip after all.

Swwww... swwww... swwww... "Here."

Quan took the blunt then got up to turn on the iPod.

Swwww... swwww... swwww... Quan hit the blunt again. Seconds later the song "I Blew a Bag Today" blared through the speakers. "Yo', I'm good and high. Put this shit out and save some for them hoe's who 'bout to come through," Quan said.

Chad nodded his head in agreement and said, "Damn, man I'm fucked up right now." Then he gazed at Quan and thought, *bitch-nigga I'll kill you.*

Quan looked up from checking his messages. "Say what, bruh?"

Chad didn't respond. He just continued to stare at him, but in his mind, he was looking right through him.

"You good, bruh?" Quan asked but Chad didn't respond.

"That nigga trippin'," Quan mumbled to himself, looking back down at his phone. *Click-clack.* Quan looked up when he heard what sounded like a gun, and realized Chad had his banger drawn and pointed toward him.

"I'll kill you, pussy-nigga. I know it was you who killed my pet frog lil' Jimmy," Chad said, sounding as if he were speaking in slow motion.

"Man, what the fuck you talkin' 'bout, crazy-ass, nigga? When you had a frog for a pet?" Quan asked.

"Shut up! Just shut up, Ne Ne. I'm the head honcho 'round this bitch. That's my pussy you sittin' on," Chad said, then pointed the gun at Quan's head.

"Man, bruh, chill the fuck out wit' that shit, you trippin'." Quan didn't know what to do so he got up and went to the kitchen to get some cold water and a rag and went back over to Chad.

Chad was having what's called an episode, caused by the synthetic marijuana which made a person dehydrated, hallucinate, and throw up till there was nothing left in their stomach.

It was 6:35 p.m when Quan threw the cold water on Chad Chad dropped the gun instantly and began growling like a dog. Then he fell on the floor and began screaming. Next, he jumped up and started running in place. "I want my bike!" he yelled over and over. Quan tried to calm him down but Chad kicked and scratched at him.

"Man, get yo' ass up and stop trippin'," Quan said, starting to panic. Chad sat up and started making a loud noise that mimicked the sound of a police siren.

Boom, Boom, Boom! There was loud knocking on the door.

"Damn!" Quan said. "There go them hoe's. Who is it?" he called out.

"Shell, Mimi and Peaches!" a female's voice said from the otherside.

He snatched the door open and pulled them in. They heard the music, but they also heard the siren sound coming from Chad.

"What the fuck," Mimi said, when she saw Chad sitting Indian style on the floor, howling away. Quan was embarrassed for his boy but he didn't know what to do for him.

Shell asked what was wrong with him and Quan told her. He also explained how he had just thrown cold water on him but it didn't work. She informed him that you're never supposed to do that because it could send a person into shock. Shell was a real RN and she explained to him how she'd seen cases like Chad's before.

"Go to the kitchen and grab him something sweet to eat," Shell said. Quan ran to the kitchen and came back with the quickness.

"We don't have nothin' sweet," Quan said.

"Alright, Mimi run to the car and grab them candy bars in the glove box, real fast." Shell began talking to Chad as if he were a gun shot patient who had been brought in the hospital on a stretcher. "It's gonna be alright, momma got you okay?"

While she used the cool rag to wipe over Chad's forehead, Mimi came back in and handed her a candy bar. Shell force fed the candy bar to Chad then made him drink some the pineapple Fanta to hydrate him. Within fifteen minutes he was back to normal.

"Man, you scared the shit outta me, bruh, wit' yo' crazy ass," Quan said. "Nigga, you pulled a gun on a nigga and er'thang. Then you went sho' nuff crazy. I had to hit you wit' the cold water and er'thang, homes." He laughed and added, "If it wasn't for these beautiful women, I don't know what I would have done, folks."

Chad didn't remember shit about the incident, and he was still woozy from the Lean. "Thank y'all, I 'preciate er'body. I'ma 'bout to go take a shower real quick then we can get this party started up," he said.

"I'm comin' wit' you," Shell said, grabbing him by his hand.

Shell was high yellow, five feet, and weighed one hundred forty-two pounds. Her breasts were a size thirty double D's, and she had, what Chad considered, a big ol' fat elephant ass, with a tiny waist. Her hair was long and wavy due to her being part Puerto Rican and part Black.

Boom! The door came crashing down.

"Nobody move! Everbody get face down on the mutha-fucken floor, now!" one of the two white boys yelled, as they pointed their guns at everybody.

"I said face down, bitch!" one of the boys said, as he kicked Mimi in the ribs with force.

"Umph," Mimi let out a moan.

"Anybody else with y'all?" the same white boy asked. No one said a word and the biggest of the white boys walked over to Quan and hit him cross his head a couple of times, with an assault rifle.

"I said . . ." *whap* "Is . . ." *whap* ... Anybody else . . ." *whap!* "In the muthafuckin' house!" *whap...*

"Nah," Chad yelled. "What the fuck y'all want, man?"

"Fuck Boy, you know what we want. Now where's it at so we can leave y'all alone?" Maliss asked.

Maliss and his partner both had on voice distorters that went over their throats, so he wasn't worried about them knowing who they were, and they also had on Real Human Disguise (RHD's) that covered half their upper bodies so they wouldn't be recognized.

"We don't have shit, white boy," Chad said.

Woom! The biggest of the white boys kicked Chad right in his mouth. "Let's try this again, bitch nigga," he said. He looked down at Chad who was bleeding profusely from the mouth. "Stop fuckin' around! *whap, whap, whap!* He hit Chad with the butt of his gun but Chad still didn't budge. He was trying to take in as much detail as possible so he could report it to his bossman and then they would kill the two crackers together.

"Alright, get your bitch-ass up," Hawk said, as he snatched Quan off the floor. "I'm tired of fuckin' around." He sat Quan in the chair and dropped kicked him in the face with his size thirteen black Timberland Boot, causing him to tumble back on the floor.

"Get the fuck up and sit back down!" Hawk shouted. Quan's vision was playing tricks on him and he was seeing flashes of different colored lights flash before his eyes. When he attempted to stand, he had a hard time getting up off the floor, so he just lay there wallowing.

"Now . . .," Hawk said. He paused momentarily and looked from Quan to Chad as he spoke, "this my last time askin' you . . . and if you lie or I ain't satisfied with your answer, I'm finna put yo' brains all over the wall, and that's on God. Now . . . do you understand?" Hawk asked. Quan nodded his head up and down.

"We been casin' this bitch for months," Hawk lied, "and we been in the area all day today watchin' all the money y'all been makin'. And from what I saw, ain't nobody left outta here except the customers and that nigga we been tryna catch drivin' that blue Vette, but the fucker drive a little too fast for us to catch up wit' him.

So, fuck it, we figured y'all could get him over here for us, or just tell us his name and when he'll be comin' back. But if not, then I guess it's lights out for er'body up in this muthafucka. Of course, we still gon' get whatever bread and drugs y'all got stashed up in here. We can do this the peaceful way and leave, or we can do it the hard way. I don't really give a fuck, on God," Hawk said in a nonchalant tone.

"Fuck you, bitch, get it in blood!" Chad yelled out.
Whap! Whap!

"Fuck me?" Maliss said, pistol whipping Chad. *Whap! Whap!* "Who is he?" *Whap!* "Where that shit at, nigga?"

The girls were crying frantically. Peaches peed on herself. "Just tell 'em," Mimi said.

"No you don't," said Shell.

"Okay, okay, okay. Just stop beatin' him. Man, I'll tell you," Quan said. "I'll tell you everything. Just promise not to kill us."

"Fuck that," Chad mumbled.

"Umm-hmm," Maliss said, preparing to whip Chad again.

"His name is Maliss, man. His name is Maliss and he come through every two days. We don't know where he stay or shit else 'bout him. I swear. The money and the dope in the back, in the closet in the safe. The numbers are 14-26-32, now just leave us alone, please," Quan pleaded.

"No, no, noooo," Chad mumbled through a broken jaw and a closed eye. "Fuck, bitch ass nigga," he continued to moan to Quan through his broken jaw.

"Now, now . . . calm down there, boy," Maliss told Chad. "If the info is right, we gon' keep our end of the bargain." He couldn't believe the double-crossing fuck-nigga crawling on his belly had sold him out like that. He wanted to reveal himself so badly but he knew he couldn't. He knew he had to keep his plan in place, and that meant eliminating all weak links.

Hawk left to go check the closet safe and came back with the merchandise. He walked it over to Quan.

"Got it," he said to his partner. "Thanks for the info you rat-ass bitch," he told Quan. "We'll be seein' you around."

Hawk walked towards Chad who was kneeling next to Mimi, then reared back so far with his foot and kicked Mimi in the head. She automatically started shaking and going into convulsions.

"Rat-ass bitch," Hawk said. He jumped on her head with both feet and applied pressure with all his two hundred forty pounds. Next, they stood in front of Chad with their guns drawn. Maliss stared at him seriously. "You a G-ass nigga"

Chad stared death right in the face and said, "Fuck you!"

"Yeah, we like you, but you should've kept better company. Look at your friend, he sold all y'all out so he clearly can't be trusted under pressure. He told on the one person who was puttin' food on his plate. You know what they say, never bite the hand that feed you, but I'll tell you what, gangster, today is your lucky day.

In order to keep your life you gon' have to take his. Or. . . you can die right along with this rat-bitch. It's all on you, playa. We already put one of them bitches down for you so what's it gone be? Live to die another day and try to get us another time? You know, do this shit like G's and keep it in the street. But, whatever you gon' to do, you need to hurry up 'cause time runnin' out."

By now, Mimi had already stopped shaking and she had also stopped breathing. Peaches was scared shitless, and Shell chose to remain quiet.

"Yeah, I wanna live to die another day," Chad said. Maliss emptied the clip on his gun then placed one of the bullets back in the chamber. He walked over to Chad, who in turn walked over to Quan and pointed the gun at his head.

"No, bruh, I was just tryna save us. Man, they were—"

Boom! Click, click, click... Chad was still pulling the trigger.

"Let's get the fuck outta here," Hawk said.

"You better move around and tighten up your security if you gon' be in the game, playboy. Cause next time that can be you," Maliss said, pointing a finger at Quan's dead body.

Hawk hit the door but not before securing the bag and making sure Maliss was straight, and then, just like that, they were gone.

CHAPTER 6

"Time to say goodnight, you burrito eatin' ass wet-back," Hawk said out loud, as he sat in his black on black Suburban LT. The Suburban was super charged up, with hidden gun compartments and dark tint.

It was 11:15 p.m. and families were pouring out laughing, seemingly having a good time, and in good spirits.

Swww, swww, swww. Hawk hit the blunt a few times. He put a Molly in his mouth and sucked on it until it disolved.

Vrrrmm, vrrmm, vrrmm...

Hawk looked to his left and saw Carlos pulling up right beside him. "I Ain't Feelin' These Niggas" by lst Degree blared through his 911 Bose Speakers:

In the heat of da night, my niggas they bound to act a nut
steady holla out what's up / killas in da cut
better duck cause we thug up
hustle mode and da murda squad killa is in da yard
watchin' out for da 30 / 40 shots in a rifle
wit' a black flag bout da blast fa survival
just call dis da tag team/ get ya team tag
when we creep in da green Jag
pullin' dro out da green bag
cruisin' through da city on my iPhone lean back

Carlos was so engrossed in the music he hadn't realized he was in danger. He sat back in his seat, bobbing his head to the beat, chilling and feeling like the boss he knew he was.

I should snatch his ass right now and be on my way, Hawk thought.

Click, clack, click, clack...

Hearing what sounded like heels clicking on the pavement, Hawk looked at his rearview and noticed a bad bitch struttin' toward his and Carlos' vehicles. Her strut was hard and she rocked a pair of six-inch Red Bottoms and wore a spaghetti-strap, fitted, Channel dress. She walked right past Hawk's truck and didn't notice him as she slid in the passenger side of Carlos' whip. Hawk looked at his watch and saw that the time was 11:41 p.m. When he looked up, he turned his attention toward Carlos and saw the same bitch giving him some mega-head.

"Just like that. Umm," Carlos moaned.

"You like that, daddy?" the girl, whose name was Sonya, asked. His only response was to push her head back down. Wow, daddy, you so big," Sonya lied, as she licked the head of his dick. *Slurp, slurp, slurp...*

The sounds of heavy breathing filled the Porche as Carlos moaned and groaned as he reached his climax. "Umph, umph, umph. Sss. Sss. Shit," he exclaimed, letting his man-juice skeet to the back of her throat. "Damn girl, you don't play. You black bitches got that fire head, no lie. Your name shoulda been lava head," he said and smiled at his own humor.

Sonya checked herself in the mirror then opened the palm of her hand to collect her bread. "I'll be whoever you want me to be for that check, baby," she said as she opened the door to get out.

"Same time, same place next week," Carlos said. "You can bet on that."

That was the quickest four bands I ever made, Sonya said to herself. She walked away just as quickly as she walked up.

Range Rovers started pulling in along with Wraith's, Ferraris, Lambos, Vipers and Corvettes. Columbians, Arabs, Asian's, Whites, black's, Puerto Rican's, and Mexican's stepped out of their rides looking like multimillionaire's.

"Damn, I need to be at Triperlett's tonight, or somethin', shit, and put trackers on all they ass, and come up." Hawk said.

"Let me see who our next vic gon' be right now, fuck all that."
At 12:00 a.m. sharp, Maliss pulled up in a F350 with a six-inch lift, on monster tires that were thirty-two inchs off the ground. "Look at my dog," Hawk said, "that boy a true bread winner.

Maliss stepped out of his hundred thousand dollar truck wearing a cream colored Tom Ford suit with the honey colored Tom Ford silk handkerchief, matching silk socks, sporting the matching honey colored, Summer Season, Tom Ford quarter-cut, alligator dress shoes. Like the old folks say: *'the boy was casket sharp'.*

"What up, long money, Maliss?" the doorman said, greeting Maliss as he patted him down for entry.

"Aww, you know me, bruh. Just hoping Ben Franklin on my side tonight. I need a blessing," Maliss replied with a friendly smile.

"So, you praying to the gambling god tonight, huh." The doorman laughed.

"1 guess you can say that." Maliss was directed to the room for the poker players.

***

From da window to da wall / to da sweat drop off my balls / to all skeet motherfucker to all skeet skeet got damn. The music blared inside The Foxy Lady strip club.

Then the DJ switched the beat, mixing it up on the turntables.

I'm gettin' my freak on / Kush got me ching chong / she playin' with my balls ping pong / I ring her bell ding dong. "Freak On, Freak On" by 1st Degree came on, and Sky came out wearing a see-through top and thong with handcuff's on it, made by Illegal Activity.

"Damn, Sky bad as a muthafucker," Lil' Fred said to Lil' Rod.

"Hell yeah, boy," Lil' Rod said. Two buckets of Corona and three bottles of Belaire Brut sat in front of him. Shirley was riding Lil' Rod cowgirl style while he stuffed one's in her garter. Lil' Fred had his finger stuffed in Summer, finger-fuckin' her with a blue hunnid dollar bill.

"You soaking wet," Lil' Fred said to Summer. She rode his finger while making her pussy muscles grip it, keeping the $100 bill inside her walls as if it were a vending machine.

"Umm-hmm, baby, this how you got me," Summer said.

"Oh yeah," Lil' Fred said.

"Yes, baby," she cooed. Lil' Rod grabbed a bottle of Belaire Brut and gave Shirley fifty dollars before he dismissed her, and then he headed to the stage where Sky was.

Fuck all that, he thought, *that's who I'm fuckin' tonight.*

As he made his way through the crowd, J-Racks and his compadres had surrounded the stage, making it rain down money. Sky slid down the pole upside down really slow with one leg holding onto the pole, shaking her huge ass.

Sky was from Greensboro, North Carolina. She'd been in Columbus, Georgia for four years, and she was the star at Foxy Lady. She was an amazon, standing six feet two inches tall, weighing in at a super thick one hundred seventy-five pounds, and toned up in all the right places. J-Racks seemed to throw tens at Sky all night, while his clique threw fives.

"I got 'em for months," J-Racks said, drunkenly, "I'll flood this bitch like God did Noah and them," he boasted. "Look at this broke ass wannabe-me," J-Racks told one of his workers when he looked over and saw Lil' Rod.

"Yeah, I see him, Boss."

J-Racks looked on and proceeded to mean-mug Lil' Rod. Lil' Rod looked in J-Rack's direction, nodded and smiled. He reached in his Gucci bag and pulled out a fist full of hundreds and threw them toward the stage at Sky. Seeing all the bills flying in the air and land on stage, she moved over, closer to where Lil' Rod was standing.

"That's what I'm talkin' 'bout, put on for daddy and you might be able to buy your first Benz off me tonight, and then let me fuck you in it, of course," Lil' Rod hollered out.

Sky was poppin' her pussy so hard in Lil' Rod's face, he couldn't throw the blue faces up fast enough.

He turned his bottle up on the niggas and yelled out, "Yo', this my pussy for the night!"

J-Racks couldn't believe it. "Damn the lil' nigga ain't bullshittin'." He ordered a twenty piece, $20,000 in ones. "I'ma make this nigga go broke in this bitch, tonight. Fuck wrong wit' him?" he told Red Dog.

Just then, another song by 1st Degree came on.

I get it in, get it out / get it in, get it out/ from da back on the side I get it in, get it out/ get it in, get out/ fuck game cost a jag/ big face in from the counter to the couch it out.

J-Racks threw fist fulls of hundreds from a platter one of his workers held for him. Seeing so much money at once caused Sky to nut on herself. She had never made that type of bread in one night, hell, not even in one month.

"My bag pretty deep, old school," Lil' Rod yelled to J-Racks over the music. Then, he reached out his hand and smacked Sky right on her big ass. "Save some of that energy for later on, now," he told her. He rolled up five hundreds with a .4 gram of Mollie, and pushed them deep inside her wetness and pulled it out slowly, before pushing them back in, making sure it was in there—this time he left it inside her. Finally, Sky's time was up, and the song went off.

"Oh my God," she said, when she looked down and then back at the stage.

"Here," Lil' Rod said, holding his hand out toward her's with a .2 of Molly. Sky crawled to the end of the stage and licked her long tongue out and swept her money in a pile. The bouncer had to bring her a trash bag because there was so much.

"Move out the way, fuck nigga," one of J-Rack's workers said, as he bumped Lil' Rod out the way.

Lil' Rod reached in his bag and came up with ten stacks. He whirled around as hard as he could and smacked him in the face with it. "That's for your doctor bill, pussy nigga." Then, he took a champagne bottle and hit him up against his head, but the bottle didn't break. He swung a second time and all hell broke loose in the Foxy Lady.

***

"This game is called, Viagara. It's a Boat or better to win, and everybody know a Boat is a full house. Two out your hand must play. It go this way or this way. Straight eight down the V, not across," Maliss said. "Boat or better," he said, as he dealt,

"Two must fit. Everybody understand?" he asked. "Aight, I'ma flip the flop first, then I'ma flip one from each side." *Vrrm, vrrm, vrrm...* His phone went off. He was down two hundred thousand dollars. He had brought A half of mil' ticket with him which was light compared to some of the competition.

"Twenty-five for the flop," the Arab said, feeling good about his hand. Since he had two Jacks in his hand, he had the 4th best hand at the table.

"I call," the Asian said.

"I call," the Puerto Rican said.

"I call," said Carlos.

"I call too," said Maliss, then he flipped the flop. It was a jack-of-hearts, an ace-of-Spade's, and a seven-of-Clubs.

They went back and forth, adding more and more money to the pot.

"Aight, pot, right?" Maliss asked the houseman.

"Yep. Pot now at a cool six hundred seventy-five thousand."

"Okay. Bet on you, champ," Maliss said, to Randy.

"Three hundred thousand," Randy said, trying to push any and everybody out of the way of his already made hand.

Carlos looked at him long and hard, then looked at Maliss. They were good. He couldn't tell who was gonna win, but he was no fool. He did have a Boat, but there were two jacks showing and two aces, which meant there was a possibility that somebody had four-of-a-kind. He had money, however, he hadn't gotten it from being dumb.

"I fold," Carlos said. "I'ma let y'all two fight it out."

"I'm aight wit' sixty racks, Randy, unless you want my watch in there too. It's worth the odds. I'm sure you know that. It's a Patek Philippe," Maliss said.

"Well, we came this far. I guess I'll give it a shot," Randy said. So, Maliss took off his watch and tossed it into the pile with the money. He just knew he couldn't lose since he had the best four-of-a-kind you could have on the board, four aces.

"Pot, right?" Maliss asked, the houseman.

"Yep, one million two hundred seventy-five thousand, to be exact."

"Aight, we can flip these out, Randy, 'cause I'm all in, partna. May the best man win," Maliss said.

"Aight, flip 'em," Randy said. It didn't even matter what the cards were because they were both made already. Randy had four-of-a-kind, jacks, and Maliss had four-of-a-kind aces.

"Damn, I could have won some of that Arab's money," Carlos said, when he saw it was a King.

"That's after poker," Randy said. "Good hand," he said to Maliss, as he reached out to shake his hand.

"Same to you, homie. You better know if I put my watch in the pot, I know I got a sure thing. It's all about the timing. Well boys, until next time, its been fun. I'm a "M" richer thanks to y'all. But like I said, better luck next time. I got my wife waiting and I'm late. Good night, gentleman," Maliss said.

"Oh, and for you men who didn't get to play, you should thank me 'cause I saved y'all some bill money," Maliss continued.

"Get yo' ass outta here with them lil' wins," somebody hollered out from the crowd.

"Lil' winnin'?" Maliss turned around and asked. "What, y'all must want to still play a few more hands and fatten my gift bag up some more or somthin'."

"Hell yeah," somebody replied.

"Let's do this then," another person cosigned.

"I ain't got shit else to do right now," another said.

"Aww, look at y'all ready to take my earnings from me," Maliss said.

"Nah, I'll pass. Catch me next week fellas," and with that, Maliss he made his departure.

"Damn, it's two-thirty already. I hope this muthafucka go straight home. Shit, I gotta cool four hours and forty-five minutes tops to get over there, strike, and get back home before princess Gabbie gets ready to go to school," Maliss said, talking to himself as he walked to his truck. He noticed Hawk was gone so he knew it was show time.

***

"Hola, señorita," Carlos said, as he entered his massive bedroom. His wife was sound asleep on, lying on her stomach. "Look at all that ass I done paid for. Umm, mmm, mm," Carlos said. His dick had started getting hard the minute he'd lay his eyes on the lovely sight.

He walked over and massaged it and gave it a firm smack. Now he was ready to fuck but knew his son was up hiding, waiting for him to come into his room and find him like always. Since he had popped two percs on the way home, he was feeling a little tired but he still made his way to his son's room.

"Alfy," Carlos whispered. He opened up his son's closet but Alfy wasn't there. "Alfy . . .," he whispered again.

"Man, this storm right on time," Hawk said to Maliss, as they waited to make their move on Carlos.

"Yeah, it couldn't have come at a better time," Maliss replied. "It's three-thirty now, so we'll give him twenty-five more minutes tops and then we'll slide up in that muthafucka. I already know he loaded wit' his salad-tossin'-eatin' ass. That nigga brought out 1.5 mill just to gamble wit'."

"This bitch gotta be crazy 'cause he ain't got no security or nothin'," Hawk said.

"Nah, 'cause he tryna be one of them sophisticated drug dealers. Dude be tryna fit in but at the same time look as normal as possible to his community. That's how they do it where they from.

They in it for the long haul for they families so they can pass on what they learned and earned to the next generation. That's why I know the money in there, 'cause they don't wanna put their money in our community. They would rather send it back to their own country. So, that's where we come in. We clean up our community, and build it up for *our* people," Maliss said.

"What's understood ain't gotta be explained," Hawk replied.

By now, Carlos had stopped searching for his son. He had looked in all his son's usual hiding places but couldn't find his son for nothing, so he had finally given up. *I'll get his little butt in the morning,* he thought. The drugs he had taken had kicked in and his eyes were starting to feel heavy, promting him to lie down and fall fast asleep. However, if he would've looked in his closet or put his money away as usual, he would've found Alfy.

"Dang, I was gonna scare dad to death with this one," Alfy, whispered. He had his Ninja turtle costume on, and he was ready to fight the bad guys. While he had been waiting on his father to find him, he'd made a pallet on the closet floor and curled up on top of it.

Moments later, he heard the door graze softly over the carpet. He eased up to the keyhole, thinking his dad was trying to trick him. He was startled when he saw two people dressed in all black, wearing ski masks over their faces like he'd seen in the movie, State Property. His little heart began to beat faster. *Dad wake up, the bad guys are her*e, Alfy thought.

Pff! Pff! Pff! The suppressor muffled the sound of the weapon.

Seconds later, Hawk hit the sleeping woman in the back of the head, cheating her out of life, sending her to an early grave. It happened so fast, she was dead instantly and never even saw death coming. Blood oozed from her head and down the side of the bed.

Alfy saw his mother's body jerk from the impact and knew something was seriously wrong. His mouth gaped open in horror. His eyes watered up. He eased over to the shoe holder and got his dad's 357, and looked inside the cylinder. When he looked back through the keyhole, he saw the masked bandit pistol whipping his father out of his sleep. *Whap, whap, whap!* "Get yo' burrito-eatin' ass up, bitch-ass muthafucka." The repeated hits were so powerful, a big gash formed on the side of Carlos' head.

"What the fuck is this!" Carlos groaned after he finally came around. His hand went to the open cash in his head.

"Bitch, this the mufuckin' bill collector," Maliss said, pointing to himself, "and this right here is the reaper," he added as he gestured toward Hawk.

"What do y'all want from me? Why are you here?" Carlos asked, remaining calm on the outside, but panicking on the inside. He wondered where his son was.

"Shut the fuck up, migo. I ask the muthafuckin' questions 'round this bitch, and *you* do the answerin'," Maliss ordered.

"Okay, okay, just don't hurt us. Man, I'll give you whatever you want," Carlos said. *Just play along*, he thought.

"Too late, wet-back. Ya' bitch is already dancin' wit' the devil."

Carlos looked over at his wife. Through the blood running down his face, he saw the bloody mess beside him. "Aww, nah man! What have y'all done? Noo, no, this can't be. What have y'all done to her? You didn't have to do that, man. I would have given y'all whatever you wanted."

Whap! "Bitch, you still gon' give us what we want. Where the money and the drugs at for starters? We want all That shit," Maliss said.

"Every damn drop!" Hawk spat, then slapped Carlos with the pistol again.

This bitch gotta be crazy outta his rabbit-ass mind if he think I'm giving up all my product, Carlos thought. "Okay, the money is downstairs in the duffel bag and that's all of it, I swear. I don't— "

Whap, whap! Maliss hit him with the speed of lighting. "Who the fuck you think you dealin' with?" he asked, as he hit him again and again. Then, he held up the duffle bag he was already holding and asked, "What, you talkin' 'bout *this* duffel bag?"

Carlos' eyes bulged out of his head and blood poured from the side of his face rapidly.

"Don't insult my intelligence," Maliss said in a stern tone.

"Man, that's all the money I have here. I-I- d-don't keep shit here," he stutterd out.

Pow! Pow! Maliss shot him in both of his legs, causing Alfy's body to jump inside the closet.

"Arrr, arrrr!" Carlos hollered out in agony.

"So, you wanna play this the hard way, huh," Maliss asked. "Aight, this is just what I expected outta you. Go grab Nightmare for me," Maliss told Hawk. Nightmare was a black Mamba snake Maliss used to torture his victims. The Mamba snake was known to release a series of bites in rapid succession, and one bite from one would release enough venom to kill at least 10,000 men.

Hawk left the room but quickly returned and handed Maliss a pillowcase. Maliss held the pillowcase up and told Carlos about the snake inside. He shook the pillowcase a little, causing the snake to become agitated.

Pow! Pow! Next, he shot Carlos in both of his shoulders, initiating him to scream out in excruciating pain.

Inside the closet, Alfy began to cry, silently. He knew his dad was getting hurt because he had heard him holler out.

"Since you wanna play games, I'ma release Nightmare in this room, leave, and close the door behind us. I guess we'll see you again in Hell," Maliss said with a straight face.

"Come on, bro, fuck him," Hawk intervened, as he ushered Maliss toward the door. They had made it all the way to the door before Carlos shouted out, pleading for them to halt.

"Okay, okay, I'll tell y'all where it's at, just don't hurt my little boy, man."

"Aight, I promise."

"It's in the closet. You have to slide the shoe case over. The combination is 18-24-7. That's everything, man. I swear it is," Carlos said, his voice pleading.

"It's on you." Maliss turned to Hawk. "Go check it out. If it's not what he says it is, it's curtains for his ass!" Maliss said, pointing the gun at Carlos' head.

Hawk went towards the closet and opened the closet door. *Boom!* came a loud explosive noise. Alfy had shot Hawk at point blank range in the chest, knocking himself to the back of the closet. The impact not only knocked Hawk back, but it also knocked him out. Luckily for Hawk, he was wearing a level three bulletproof vest, otherwise, it would've been curtains for him.

The gun sounding off scared the shit out of Maliss, and it caused him to pull his own trigger, putting three right in Carlos' head. He ran over to the closet and Alfy had already dropped the gun from his hands due the recoil. Without hesitation, Maliss shot the little boy two times, back to back—one in the chest and one in the head. He picked Alfy up, and as if he were nothing more than a rag doll, flung him out of the way. Then he proceeded to the ten-feet tall shoe case which was really the safe.

"Come on, come on,"Maliss coached himself. He knew he had to hurry up, especially since he was in the suburbs part of the city. He was sure somebody had heard the gunshots and the police were probably already en route.

It was 4:40 a.m., when Maliss put the code in the safe. *Swoosh!* it opened up, as the pressure was relieved from the vacuum sealed door. The safe was *loaded*.

"Fuck!" he said, as he reached up and snatched a bed sheet down from the shelf. He began pulling and pouring money in the sheet with the speed of an expert. After he tied the sheet up, he pulled another one down and started loading that one with bags and bags of percs and K2.

"Damn!" he said, after noticing what had been hidden behind the percs ard K2. Stacked as tall as the safe itself, there were bricks of ice, Molly and heroin. The safe was four-feet deep.

He tied the last sheet up and dragged two of them down to the front door then ran back upstairs for two more. Hawk was still knocked out. After getting the bags to the door, Maliss ran to the kitchen to find some flammable house supplies. He placed them in the microwave and set the heat to twenty minutes. Then, he took off to get Hawk. When he got back up the stairs, Hawk was just starting to come around.

"Come on, homes," Maliss said to Hawk.

"Hmm, Hawk moaned from the pain he was feeling in his chest.

"Come on, we gotta get outta here, killa. Now get your big ass up." Maliss strained to get Hawk to his feet as the loud sound of sirens whirled in the background.

"Let's go, let's go, unless you wanna spend the rest of your life in a jail cell." His last comment seemed to motivate Hawk because he began to move at a steady pace, as if to say *'fuck this pain'*.

The two men tore the stairs up two at a time, grabbing the sheets on the way out.

When they reached the truck, they threw the sheets on the back and pulled off the block really slow, with the lights still off.

The sirens from the police cars were getting closer, and as soon as they turned off the street, twelve patrol cars pulled up on the scene from the opposite direction.

The wet pavement from the pouring rain caused the wheels to screech as the cars slid to a stop.

"You take the back, we'll cover the front," the Lieutenant ordered. The officers rounded the back as the lieutenant headed for the front door.

"Police, anybody home! Police, is there anybody—

BOOM! The house exploded and went up in flames.

***

It was 6:00 a.m. and Lil' Rod and Sky were just leaving the Ramada Inn on Highway 280. "When we gon' do this again? I'm tryna hit you and your homegirl, Lil Red, next door. So, what that ticket gone be, for real? For real we can do something tonight if you can set it up. Just give me the time and the place," Lil' Rod said.

"Let me see. I'ma call her later and when I find out the price we can go from there," Sky said, as they walked to her *Skurrrt!* Tires screeched and an all black SS Camaro stopped in front of them. A nigga jumped out before Lil' Rod could pull out his strap.

"Go for it, I dare you pussy-ass-nigga. Both of yall get the fuck on the ground, and give me this," the mask man demanded, simultaneously snatching Lil' Rod's Cuban link chain off his neck. Then, he took his gun out of his waist.

He snatched Sky and Lil Rod's car keys, then slung Lil Rod's keys as far as he could throw them. Next, he deactivated

Sky's alarm and jumped in the driver's seat, before 9pulling off with her entire life savings.

"No, no, noo," she screamed, as she watched the car get farther and farther out of sight. The masked man was far from worried about the Camaro since it had been stolen anyway. Needless to say, Lil Rod' was heated.

CHAPTER 7

DJ DNT Panic was in the lab putting a track together for 1st Degree to smash.

"Hell yeah, boy. I like that already," 1st Degree said. "Put some organs in that bitch and a electric guitar, bruh. I think I already got something for that shit," he said, playing with his voice freestyling over the sneers.

Money make you handsome, even when you ugly. . . 1st Degree's phone came to life as the sounds of Gucci Mane rang out.

"Yo', turn that down some," 1st Degree said to DJ Panick. Once he saw the caller ID display the incoming call as an unavailable number, he pressed send, the option to answer.

"You have a prepaid call from: City Boi Freak. You will not be charged if you press 1. If you accept the charges, press 5." He pressed 5 to accept. *This call is being recorded and is subject to monitoring. Your call has been connected. You may begin speaking now . . ."*

"Boi, this you?" 1st Degree answered. "What's up?"

"Man, where my birthday cards at?" City Boi Freak asked. His tone was agitated but his disappointment was evident.

City Boi Freak was a big time D-Boi from Dothan, Alabama. Back in the day, he had a studio and a club called 360. He and 1st Degree had met during a work release in Alexander City, Alabama. The two hooked up after they'd gotten released. City Boi Freak became his manager and the two worked together until the Feds picked him up on a conspiracy drug charge. The government attached an 851 enhancement to his charge which resulted in him being given a life sentence.

"I ain't made it to the post office yet, bruh, but I got everything ready for you," 1st Degree told him.

"Man, I need my cards, nigga. And I'm ready to see them hoes, too, bruh. Damn, what's takin' so long?" City Boi Freak said.

"I got you ol' school. Calm down, nigga. Did you even check your account?" 1st Degree asked him.

"Man, damn that, I wanna hear my name at mail call, nigga. Gon' handle that, bruh."

"This call is being recorded and subject to monitoring," the recording repeated over the call.

"I got you, bruh. I just been busy with my career, my nigga. I'm on a fifty-two city, Black Lives Matter tour, right now, as we speak. I'm in the Yoe right now on the bus," 1st Degree said.

"That mean you got fifty-two chances to send my shit, hell," City Boi Freak said, laughing.

"Man, sit back nigga. I got you, but where my little change at anyway since you wanna talk that shit? You don't need shit. I'm already knowin' you straight in there. Who you think you talkin' to? Nigga you just tryna put on. I'm out here pavin' the way for us so we can be straight when you touch down. You'll be able to have whatever you want. Me, Cuz, and Big Boi gon' make it happen. So, fall back and keep your nose clean, so you can get your old ass ready to fuck some of these bad ass hoes on the road."

"Alright," City Boi Freak said to First Dagree. "Paper Boi, put my Mp3 on the charger for me, bruh!" City Boi Freak, yelled out.

"Boi, I hear that shit in the backgroud. Turn that shit up, bruh," City Boi Freak said.

"A'ight, hold on." First Degree told the DJ to turn up the volume.

"Oh ni! Paper Boi come here real fast." City Boi Freak called his partner. "This my right here." He told Paper Boi Rari, who was an artist trying to get on, himself.

"Oh ni! First Degree, I got a couple of your songs on the mp3, nigga," City Boi Freak said. The song 'I aint feeling these niggas' came on. A minute later, the phone beeped, alerting him that he only had one minute left. "Look, bruh, my celly go hard too, and I want you to check him out," City Boi Freak said.

"Man, no new friends," 1st Degree shot back. "Call back in an hour, bruh."

"Go to the post office today!" City Boi Freak reiterated.

Just then, the sirens sounded off in the background.

"Lockdown, lockdown!" the officers yelled.

"Man, damn, the deuces done sounded. These bitch-ass niggas always fuckin' shit up. It's all love, bruh," City Boi Freak said.

"What? Them niggas in there fightin' again?" 1st Degree asked.

"Hell yeah,"City Boi replied. "Man, I gotta g— "

Click. The phone went dead and all that was left was the dial tone.

"Damn, I'll be glad when bruh come home," 1st Degree mumbled.

3 hours later. . .

"Aye, what happened?" City Boi Freak asked Officer Doszer, as he passed by making his rounds. Doszer was from Enterprise, Alabama.

"Man, they just stabbed a Mexican down in F-Block. He was unresponsive and they had to call in the helicopter," Officer Doszer said.

"What! Man . . . this shit crazy. How long we gon' be down you think?" City Boi Freak asked.

"Ain't no tellin'," the officer answered honestly. "Maybe two weeks, if not more." He walked off.

"Man, damn! This crazy shit ain't for me." *Lord, please release me Father God. I wanna be wit' my family Father God. I wanna be with my family. God, You know my heart and my soul Father God, Amen.* "I'm tellin' you, Paper Boi," Freak said, after he had finished praying, "If you don't learn nothin' else, bruh, you better learn to hold your own, my nigga. Take care of your family and give back to the community, lil homey. Don't take this shit for granted. You better look around and get in touch with life, period."

"Yeah bruh," Paper Boi Rari said, "I got you," he replied. He turned his attention back toward the mission at hand as he sacked up one hundred Spice papers, aka K-2, to sale once the door popped after lockdown. In the meantime, he smoked on one himself.

"You need to quit smokin' that shit," City Boi Freak lectured. "If only you knew how you look."

"Yeah nigga, I should look high. Fuck you talkin' 'bout?" Paper Boi said.

"Nah, you look junked out, my nigga. You a player, my nigga. Coming up in here talkin' all that big money talk, I knew it, I knew it. All I had to do was wait 'cause time will always reveal the true light. That's one thing my daddy always taught me and he ain't been wrong yet," City Boi Freak said. "Look at you."

"What, what happen?"

"What happen? *You* happened, fuck you talkin' 'bout. You need to get sure money while you round here bullshittin'," Paper Boi said.

"Umm..." Paper Boi stuttered.

"Umm?" City Boi Freak said. "Bruh what the fuck was that? What, you need to learn how to talk now? You too old for that *unmn* shit. Lighten yo' ass up 'round here, tryna make a nigga look bad. Everybody you fuck wit' gettin' money except you. You 'round here high talkin' 'bout, *umm*. How you think that look?"

Paper Boi Rari didn't respond.

"Now, you ain't got nothin' to say. You say you gettin' money, but I ain' seen nothin'!" City Boi Freak swung Paper Boi Rari's locker door open. It looked like he had just come in off the bus. The only thing he had in his locker was a couple of letters and a prison handbook. He didn't have a single commissary item.

"You sad, bruh, no lie," City Boi Freak said, "but I got love for you nigga. Boy you know I ain't gon' have you 'round my people like that. Get right or get left." City Boi Freak left it at that and lay back down to study his Bible, something he did everyday.

"Paper Boi!" Git called out from underneath the door, two cells down.

"Yeah!" Paper Boi hollered back.

"One time for the one," Git screamed out, then laughed.

Paper Boi and Git were both high as hell, and they always seem to be in tune with one another:

"What up with it, Git," Paper Boi said, underneath the door. "Fuck with me one time. I'ma send you one so we can mix and match and go to Pluto."

"Aight, send your line. I got my space helmet on."

"Oh ni, Paper Boi," Oowhop said, from across the hall. "Let me get four for three books," Oowhop said, referring to the currency of the Federal system, which at the time was postage stamps— three books was equal to ten dollars on the streets.

"Aight, send your line," Paper Boi said.

City Boi Freak shook his and said, "You'll get it together sooner or later, little bruh." Paper Boi didn't bother to respond.

CHAPTER 8

First Dagree had dropped a fire track, compliments of DJ DNT Panic. *Fuck Da Law* went viral. Industry heads were in an uproar over it. And the track was being talked about on every entertainment station.

"Rapper First Dagree is getting maximum exposure. It seems, his single, Fuck Da Law has grabbed the attention of the whole nation," the televisionannouncer reported. "Fuck Da Law! They're protesting in Texas. Fuck Da Law, Fuck Da Law! in Cali."

"Man, they talking bout me on T.V.," First Degree said, when the news caught his attention while he was in the studio about to record another song.

"Fuck Da Law in Boston. Everywhere you go they're playing Fuck Da Law by First Degree. This Natasha with an public announcement."

"Dang dog! Did you hear that?" First Degree asked DJ DNT Panic.

"Hell yeah, we on our way boi," DJ DNT Panic said.

First Degree changed the channel as soon as the story went off. While searching for more stories about his music, he came across breaking news of three people being killed by an explosion in a house that burnt to the ground.

"The investigation is still ongoing and no names have been released due to the fact that officials are still trying to contact the family members. From the looks of it, the neighborhood where it happened appeared to be well kept. No one seems to know anything, but a few people did say they heard gun shots and called the police.

That's all we have for now, but we'll keep you updated if any new information becomes available. If anyone has any information about the incident, please contact the number at the bottom of your screen. That number is 1-800-crimes. This is Tracy Mac reporting live from Gwinnett, Georgia. Now, back to you, Robin."

"Coming up next is the weather report from meteorologist, Mole. This is Robin Meldows reporting live, stay tuned."

"Damn, there's some foul ass people out there, boy," First Degree said. He turned the TV off and got back inside the booth. "Yo', I think I'ma name this one Street Justice."

***

Maliss dropped Hawk off at his crib, and then he made it home just in the nick of time to see how Princess off to school. Princess Gabbie kissed Maliss on the cheek. "Love you Daddy, Love you, Mommy."

"We love you, too, babe," they said, almost in unison. Princess Gabbie took off running toward the bus and seconds later she was off to school.

"Go to the room of pleasure. I got a surprise for you, bae," Ayesha said.

"Aight. Let me hit the shower real fast, then I'll be right on in there."

"OK, bae. Don't keep me waiting. I might start without you," she said. Flirtatiously, she began winding her hips and then she touched herself seductively, turning the two of them on.

After I put this wet-wet on him, he gon' say yes to whatever I ask him, she thought. A wide smile spread across her face as she made her way to the second master bedroom to freshen up.

Maliss grabbed a bottle of eight-hundred dollar Can't Ban a Jack Boi cologne and lotion, and a pair of four hundred dollar silk boxer briefs all by Illegal Activity, and headed down to the room of pleasure.

The room of pleasure was a room he had designed, filled with all types of sex toys. There were several types of liberators in all sizes, nipple clamps, and a doggie-style machine that locked her forearms down, and moved her ass backwards at a certain speed. He could control the speed as he wanted to. There was a sex swing, handcuffs, leg cuffs, whips, and a video recorder. The whole room was mirrored, but the front wall was reversed so they could see out with a view of the street, but no one could see in.

The room had all kinds of costumes from Illegal Activities including a Baby Face Nelson costume which came with a Thompson automatic and hundred round drum. He had a Purple Label Polo suit with the croch cut out, with a twenty thousand dollar stack of counterfeit bills he could replace with real money.

There was a 1896 bottle of Scotch, and a female bankteller's suit complete with a mini-skirt and blouse with one of the buttons missing from it.

Ayesha waited in the room of pleasure with her surprise wearing an all pink one-piece, black trimmed lingerie nightie with the croch cut out and matching six-inch pumps. Wearing her favorite fragrance, Pussy Cat, she knew she was irresitable.

"I hope you're ready 'cause I'm finna tear that ass up," Maliss said as he entered the room, sitting on a Liberator while watching one of their homemade sex movies on the 90-inch screen.

"This is Melanie, bae. She'll be joinin' us in our festivities today," Ayesha said. "This is my gift today, a life filled with joy and full of surprises," she went on to explain.

Ayesha liked girls on the flipside and would share in the pleasure with Maliss whenever she was in the mood. Maliss smiled and acknowledged Melanie but didn't say a word.

Ayesha looked toward Melanie and said, "Before we get started, these are the rules . . . you can suck his dick, put your mouth anywhere you want except his lips and ass.

Understand, you are only here to assist me in bringin' him to maximun pleasure. You *cannot* put *his* dick inside you," she said. "But I have dildos in all sizes right there," she said, pointing her index finger toward the dildos, "and you're welcome to use any of them you choose.

And even though you here to participate, none of this is for your benefit, and we not in it to bring you pleasure; however, you more than welcome to pleasure yourself," she went on, as if she were the teacher and Melanie was her student. "You can do the works to me, meaning, don't leave nothin' out."

Ayesha patted Melanie on her knee and Melanie nodded her head in agreement, smiling lustfully at Maleek.

"Now, Maleek, you know there ain't no kitty lickin' or intercourse, but you can touch her anywhere you want," she instructed as she gently rubbed her hands across Maleek's dick, which was already as hard as a rock.

"Uh-huh," he replied.

"Okay, anybody got any more questions before we get started," Ayesha asked.

"Yeah I do," Maliss said.

"Okay, what?" Aysha asked.

"Why didn't you ask me if I wanted to fuck, um, Melanie?" he asked her.

"Because, I already said you wasn't goin' to," she said with a slight attitude and a roll of her neck.

"But you said this was a gift for me," Maleek debated. "And I —

"Yes, *and I* already gave you my rules, take it or leave it, nigga," Ayesha cut him off. Melanie crossed her legs tightly as the first nut of many coursed through her body. Just hearing him say he wanted to fuck her made her pussy jump. She was turned on by everything about him—from the smell of his

76

expensive cologne to his six-pack abs and super toned body, right down to his long, massive size dick.

"If there's nothin' else, let's proceed please."

Ayesha got up and strutted over to the stereo and put on "Freak Me" by Jodeci, then she adjusted the lights and set the recorder. "You did sign the contract to be recorded, right?" she asked Melanie.

"Yes," Melanie answered. She watched Maleek change into his Neal Armstrong costume with the two spam helmets, with the trademark Illegal Activity signature on them. She blushed as he walked over to her, ready for her oral preformance.

Let me lick you up and down till you say stop . . . The song played softly through the speakers and Maleek laid down on the big Liberator that curved into an S shape, letting his near perfect body elevate as his middle sank in and his legs rose. It was perfect for many different positions, but this one was made perfectly for getting his face rode and his dick sucked at the same time.

"Umm, I missed you, baby,"Ayesha purred as she went down on the head greedily, real tight and wet with no hands. She went down deeper and deeper, all the way to his nut sack, then Melanie began to suck his dick intensely. Their lips touched as she lay in the 69 position so he could suck her pussy at the same time.

"Let me lift the shield up, bae," Maliss said. "Now, let me take it off for a minute. Okay, yeah, now that's better."

Ayesha moaned and stared into Melanie's eyes with pure pleasure on her face while she mouth-massaged her man extra slow. Maliss' toes were curled tightly as he licked and sucked Ayesha's waxed pussy and watched it on the 40-inch plasma bolted to the ceiling.

"Ooh, yeah," Maliss said, as Ayesha got back on the dick and sped up her rhythm. He rose up, meeting her in mid-stride. "Damn, bae," he moaned. "That's right, suck that dick."

She came up for air and grabbed him with two hands, blowing on the head of his dick lightly She leaned toward him and took him in her mouth aggressively, sucking so hard her jaws sank in on his dick.

"Ohh, shit! Hold up for a minute," He said, feeling his climax building. Melanie kept up the oral assault while Ayesha climbed on his face. Holding onto his locks, she commenced to riding his tongue as if she was a jockey in the Kentucky Derby.

"Yes, yes, yes! Ohh, baby, I'm cummin'," Ayesha said loudly, as she released all her juices in Maliss' mouth—not missing a beat he lapped up every drop like a deprived puppy. The sounds of his moaning was all that could be heard throughout the room as Melanie swallowed his seed and sucked him back bone-hard. Ayesha recouperated and lifted herself up off his face.

Maliss grabbed his helmet from the floor and dropped the shield. "Put the strap on," he told Melanie. "I want you to help me fuck the shit outta her."

He lay down on the loveseat with his leg over the armrest. "Come here, Ayesha. Put your chest on mine," he directed her. She straddled him and slid down slowly, until she had all of him deep inside her. She looked as if she was riding a real thorough bred, in fact, she was.

"Now, Melanie, I want you to squat behind her and put it in her ass. Hold her at the bottom of her waist for support. Ease in her slowly, don't tear my shit up," he ordered her sternly.

Melanie smiled. "I got this," she said, and slid all the way in. "Aww, shh-shit," Ayesha moaned out as Melanie found her way in through the back. Maliss was already so deep, she could feel the pressure in her guts.

"Ohh, bae, you so tight and wet. Gotdamn, Maliss whispred in her ear. "You got some good pussy, bae. You know that?" he asked her.

"Ye-yes, bae . . Ahhh damn!" she yelled out as Melanie locked her feet against the armrest and pressed down on Ayesha's ass, pumping her long and hard. "Ohhh lawd, yes, Jesus!" Ayesha screamed. "I'm cummin' yes, bae. I'm cummin'!"

"I ain't finished yet. Get up, bae," Maliss said. "Get up, Melanie," he told her. Melanie slid out of Ayesha gently and cleaned the strap off but kept it on. He proceeded to hold Ayesha with both of his arms locked around her back and began throwing the dick on her.

"Yesss, baby! Right there!" Ayesha screamed out. Maliss stopped and got up. "Come on over here," he told her, leading her to the doggy-style bench. Once there, he strapped her in by the forearms. "Come here, Melanie," he gestured to her. "Put it in her pussy, then lean over and put your arms underneath her stomach while I handcuff your hands together. Then, I'ma gonna turn the machine on so that it moved slowly. Next, I'ma enjoy some more of that fire head, okay?" Maliss said.

"Okay," Melanie said.

He did all that and turned the machine on, allowing Ayesha to enjoy the feeling while the machine did all the work. He then put his dick in Ayesha's mouth and grabbed her by the back of her head to fuck her mouth slow and steady.

Standing on his toes, Ayesha slurped him up. "Godleee, bae," he muttered as he stare Melanie directly in her eyes. Melanie moaned as she entered into another climax. She imagined that Maliss' dick was going in and out of her instead of fucking Ayesha's mouth.

Next, he pulled himself from Ayesha's mouth and stuffed the ball with the strap in its place, preparing her for what was next. Now, she could see the 90-inch clearly as Melanie continued to fuck her.

He walked behind Melanie with the whip and struck her tenderly across the ass. She hollered out, and at the same time, her pussy began to squirt. He struck her again and again, and again she hollered from sheer ecstasy. He pulled her by her hair and ran his dick as far up in her as he could get it, plunging it over and over as if he were a mack truck trying to bulldoze a wall.

"Sss, shit, uh, yes, more," she moaned. "I'm cumming! Oh God, I'm cumming," she yelled.

Hearing the sounds of Melanie's pleasure caused Ayesha to attempt to say something, however, her words were muffled due to the gag. Her eyes were wide with jealousy and anger.

Maliss quickly pulled out and shot his load all over Melanie's back. "Damn . . . that shit snappin'," he said out of breath. "I'm sorry, bae, but I wear the pants in this house," he said to Ayesha. She just stared at him angrily with watery eyes. "And besides, bae, I wanted to test drive this car. In the streets and in the house of pleasure, I'm Maliss, and Maliss stands for the desire to cause pain, injury, or distress. You make sure you remember that."

He released Melanie and she fell to the floor, knees weak. He released Ayesha, and as soon as she gathered herself, she swung on him instantly. She didn't even bother to unhook the gag. She threw wild, wide blows at Maliss, as he bear-hugged her in an attempt to control her.

"It's okay, bae. It's okay," he said, calmly in her ear trying to soothe her." She was way too fired up from the sex to put up a fight. So, she laid her head on his shoulder and wept silently. Maliss unhooked the gag and kissed her long and hard until her body gave in lovingly. "I still got a surprise for you, bae," she said.

"I love you and 'preciate the gift," he finally said with a smile on his face. She hit him in the chest and returned a smile of her own.

Then, she looked at Melanie with hatred in her eyes. "Get out, bitch, your servics are no longer needed," she told her. "Your money is right there on the table," she said, pointing toward the twenty-five hundred dollars. She turned her focus toward Maliss. "I want to go see my mother and father for the back home Sunday, if you don't mind, bae," Ayesha said.

"For the whole weekend?" he questioned her.

"Yeah, bae. We ain't been down there in a while," Ayesha said.

Maliss was quiet for a second. *That would be a good idea*, he thought, *I need to handle a few things out of town myself.* "Alright, bae. Come on." He grabbed her hand and led her outside. "Surprise!" he shouted.

"Surprise what?" Ayesha asked, looking around but not seeing anything.

"What, you cut the grass or something?" she asked.

Maliss laughed and revealed the set of keys he'd been hiding behind his back.

"What them go to?" she asked and took off to the garage.

"Oh my God, you didn't!" she exclaimed, sitting inside the garage looking at a pink AMG 63 G-wagon with 5 percent tint all the way around. He had it sitting on 26-inch black Forgie rims with the pink lip. "I love it, bae."

"Ohh wee, that's my truck, Dad, "Gabbie said from behind them. She had just gotten off the school bus.

"Come here, babygirl," he said. He picked her up and hugged her tightly.

"No princess, this is mommy's truck. When you get big enough daddy got you."

"Okay, daddy. Mommy, can I drive your truck then?"

"We'll see, baby," Ayesha told her, tearful from the excitement.

"Yay, mommy said we'll see, daddy," Gabbie said, as they walked inside the house.

CHAPTER 9

"You have fifty-two voice messages. Press 1 to hear your messages or press 2 to delete your messages."

Beep. Maliss pressed the end option. "This nigga probably going nuts by now. Look at all these missed calls and messages he left on my shit." *They got blood on that money and I still count it...*

BEEP!

Chad rolled over and answered his phcne. "Yo," he said through a wired mouth. "Why you blowing up my phone like this, and why you sound like that?" Maliss asked.

"My jaw wired," Chad said in a muffled tone.

"Yo' what?"

"My jaw, my jaw," he managed to say. "We had a 1320 yesterday," Chad informed him.

Maliss' phone vibrated as a text message came through. "I see," he said. "So, where y'all at now?" Maliss inquired. Unbeknowst to Chad, he was well aware of the events that had taken place.

Chad: ain't no we. that nigga gone 4ever but I'm at the Ramada in Riverdale. Chad texted, because it was painful for him to talk.

Maliss: What number?

Chad: 214

"I'll be through after a while. I'm tied up right now," Maliss said.

"Aight," Chad munbled. Maliss hit the *end* button and laid back for some rest. "It's been a long night and seems like it's gon' be an even longer morning," Maliss said to himself, before drifting off to sleep.

***

"Damn, da Rari hard," Lil' Fred said to Monkey Wrench Joe, "what that bitch go for, boy?" He inquired about a Ferrari, as he entered the repair shop.

"This old thing? Well, when we finish it'll probably go for a cool hundred," Monkey Wrench Joe said.

"I can see myself rollin' in that bitch now, nigga. The whole city gon' be on a nigga dick, boy," Lil' Fred said.

"So, what brings you to the repair shop today, Lil' Fred?" Monkey Wrench Joe asked. The term *repair shop* was their code word for chop shop.

"Well, I got a 2018 Mazzi truck, and I know I should be able to get at least forty-five for it," Lil' Fred said.

"I'ma tell you right now, hell nah. You better sell that shit on the street if you want that much for it. Them shits don't go for nothin' but eighty bands, brand new, homie. What, you tryna get old Monkey Wrench Joe or something?"

"Nah, man. I'm just sayin', hell . . . I don't know but it gotta be worth something," he said.

"Hey, Git, come here right fast." Monkey Wrench Joe called one of his mechanics over before turning back to Lil' Fred. "Where is it ?" Monkey Wrench Joe asked him.

"Out front," said Lil' Fred.

"Yeah, what's up, Monk?" Lil' L said, coming into the shop.

"Go bring that truck up in here, double time," Joe said.

"Alright, alright. I got it. Where the key at?" Lil' L asked.

"They in the truck, playa," Lil' Fred said.

"Aye, bruh, I want that Ferrari, man. Maybe we can do a trade and some cash with the truck, you feel me?" suggested Lil' Fred.

Monkey Wrench Joe was a backyard, country boy, con-artist straight out of Monroeville, Alabama. He had scheming the whole time on Lil' Fred. When he heard him say what type of truck it was, he'd already decided not to pay more than eight grand, which would be a basement bargain. His method of doing business was to buy cheap and sell high.

Lil' Fred had fifteen bands from the Cuban link money on him. *Shit, I'm finna pay for this bitch today and cnne back and pick it up this weekend.*

***

Lil' Rod rode low on the westside of Sin City in a black Viper, searching high and low for J-Racks and his workers.

"Bitch-ass niggas gotta a lot of balls robbin' me and lettin' me live. That was his first and last mistake, and everybody 'bout to get a dirt nap, complements of Draco."

He clenched his ratchet tightly. He cruised up and down the streets since it was the first time he had brought the whip out. He was just about to head south when he noticed a bright shimmer. He looked to his right, and to his surprise, he saw his chain on another nigga's neck, shining brightly in the sun.

That's BoBo, he thought. He turned the music down and sat up in the seat to get a better look. Turning off 14th Street, he drove in behind Riverview Projects and pulled his mask on.

"Stop, BoBo," Falesha said. BoBo had grabbed her from behind and pressed his hard-on against her ass. "Don't be grabbin' me like that. I'ma tell your girl, Katie," she threatened.

"Girl look at these little ass shorts you got on," he replied, reaching behind her for another feel.

Kaboom! The sound of the assault rife thundered loudly. "Bitch-ass nigga," Lil' Rod yelled as he let loose. "Fuck-nigga you took my chain. Come here, nigga!" BoBo ducked low and Falesha took off running.

Lil' Rod caught up to him, snatched him up by his dreads and pulled him toward the trunk of his car. BoBo cried and curled up as he was struck repeatedly across the head with the butt of the rifle.

"Okay, man, okay. What the fuck I do," BoBo cried out.

"Bitch-nigga, get in the fuckin' trunk!" Lil' Rod demanded before striking him again and knocking him out. "Damn," he said out loud. He sat the rifle aside to lift BoBo up off the ground then he threw him inside the trunk. He slammed it closed and got in the car and sped off.

***

"Nigga open the door and stop looking through the peephole, wit' yo' scary ass,"Maliss said, as he waited for the chain to be unlatched fom the other side.

"Gotdamn," he said once the door swung open. Chad's head was the size of a watermelon. "Damn, boy, you aight? I mean, what the fuck. I hope you aight. Who you think behind this?" Maliss asked. He was having a hard time showing concern without laughing.

Chad reached for a pad and pen to write everything down. Due to his jaw being wired he really couldn't talk. He wrote on the paper, scribbling that the perpatrator looked white but sounded black. Then, he handed the paper to Maliss.

Maliss looked it over. *At least he knows the description,* he thought.

Chad began to write again. This time he wrote down how Quan had snitched and how he ended up having to kill him in order to save his own life.

Maliss took the paper and read it quietly, concluding. *That's a good suggestion. Even I didn't think he would think line that* "You could be right," he said to Chad.

Chad nodded, then wrote: *Man, they hit us for everything, big bruh. But I got enough stashed away to cover the losses.* He handed Maliss the paper, then began writing again: I been grinding. I'm trying to open my own funeral home, you feel me? Niggaz die everyday. I can make a killing off of killings.' Chad ended the quote with a smiley face and handed the paper to Maliss.

Maliss chuckled. "Man, just give me half of what was left from the first batch, feel me. We can charge the rest of it to the game. Fuck it, losses come with the game, lil' homie. We gonna move locations, tighten up security, and keep the same formula, ya' dig," Maliss said.

Chad immediately began scribbling on the pad: I had some company over. They killed one of the girls because she was shaky, but they let the other two live. I'm fuckin' one of them. She's an RN. That's who's taking care of me for now, and her homegirl seems cool. He passed it to Maliss.

"Good. Do you trust them?"

So far so good, Chad wrote.

"Don't trust no one, nigga. They'll cut your throat to the bone so always keep your eyes open," Maliss said. "As long as you got to keep your life, you won. You didn't fail," he told Chad, passing on some words of wisdom to strengthen his spirits since he'd been beaten so badly.

Maliss' phone vibrated as a text came through. He looked it over quickly then looked up at Chad. "I have to go, but remember, only a man accepts responsibility for his actions and doesn't try to pass the blame on to someone else. If you try to do something and fail at it then you learn from your mistakes.

Failure is not the worst thing that can happen, but quitting is. These qualities and characteristics are what help make men, men. With that being said, I'm gone. You chill and hurry up and get your health back, you heard," Maliss said, giving the man a fist pound. Chad nodded and returned the dap.

"Do you need anything before I go?" Chad shook his head no.

"Aight, come lock this shit up, partna, and get well soon," Maliss said, as he made his exit. Chad closed the door and Maliss could hear several chains being locked.

CHAPTER 10

"Atlanta Federal Building 9:15 am Friday, May 26, 2020, Joam Jackson, twenty-two years old was found dead at the Holiday Inn in Jonesboro, Georgia. The cause of death was an overdose and traces of fentanyl was discovered in her system. Randy Mills, twenty-six years old has been charged with first-degree murder and released on a two hundred fifty thousand dollar bond. No court date has not been released," Agent Malone read from an Atlanta Journalist newspaper.

Agent Patricia shook her head in digust and said, "Stupid ass drug dealers."

"I hope the bitch gets the death penalty," Agent Malone said. "Donald Trump needs to keep pushing the issue. Listen to this," Maloneo continued to read from the paper. He sat behind his desk at the Federal Building in Atlanta while sipping on his second cup of coffee, "19 year old Quanathan Liles was found dead in a house fire on Old National and Godby Road. An autopsy report indicated that he died from a gunshot wound to the head prior to the fire. There was also a 20-year-old, Katrina Jones, found dead in the same house. An autopsy showed that there was trauma to the skull. Authorities believed she was actually dead before the fire started. Fire Marshalls have determined the fire was caused by lighter fluid and a match. As of now there are no witnesses or suspects," Malone read aloud.

"Old National and Goby Road?" Agent Patricia asked.

"Yeah."

"Well, isn't that the same area we keep getting reports about heavy drug activity going on?" she asked him.

"Yeah, I believe you're right. I bet you Maleek's involved in this some how," Agent Malone said.

"You think so? But how?" she asked.

"I don't know yet but I'ma figure it out, and I bet you a hundred dollars to a bucket of shit—

Before he could finish, he was interrupted by a knock on the door and Agent Gills stuck his head in the door. "I have them specs back on that tracker like you asked, sir," he said, handing Malone a single sheet of paper.

Malone examined the paper while sipping on his coffee. Serial number 422-8111-091 was distributed at Universal Spy's off highway 85 exit 13, which was located in Adamsville, Southwest Atlanta.

"Okay, Patricia, we got some action. Let's roll, babe," he said.

***

Let me find out/ let me find out/ shootin' up everywhere you hidin' out. A track by Doe B bumped in the car as Maliss pulled up at Lenox Mall in ATL.

"Get in, partna," Maliss called out and pulled off before the door could fully close.

"Damn, bruh, you got this bitch hooked all the way up. What you got in here, a LS7?" Roe Black said, looking around the interior of Maliss' whip for proof of the speakers.

"None of your damn business. Just know that it's equipped for any situation I might find myself in. But what's up with you? What makes you think you ready for a taker's lifestyle, huh?" Maliss asked. He was trying to see if Roe Black was a natural born robber like himself.

Roe was a 24-year-old drifter and he kept his personal life private. He was superhood so no one ever questioned it since he had adapted to his surroundings so well.

"Well, I used to run with the Flathead Boys. That shit was straight. I learned a lot but it wasn't enough for me. I love super nice shit. You know, the luxury life . . . so I figured I could get in with that fire-flame spitter," Roe Black said.

"Okay, I see. But what made you pursue me on such a delicate topic, not knowing me from a can of paint?" Maliss asked. He knew the streets talked, as they say, but being in the business that he was in, too much talk was dangerous.

"Well, bruh, this the streets, and I always keep my ear to the streets, feel me? Word in the streets is that you got that work, partna. And with the smarts I got I always go for the top of the food chain, and with that I'm bound to get fed, you feel me? I'm a risk-taker, so I figured if what the streets saying is true 'bout you, then I know you can guide ne in the right direction. See, I figured that if it's true there got to be some bad business somewhere, and maybe you could, like, hire me or something to clean shit up for you on that tip. Or find me a position to fill and, in return, you have my loyalty and trust forever."

"Hmm, I see. So, what makes you think I needed a position filled?" Maliss asked, keeping his eyes on the road.

"I never said you needed it. I said maybe you could find one for me. No man can do everything by himself. So where you can't, you pay someone else who can. Feel me, homes?" Roe Black said.

"Let me lace you up right quick, lil' homie. Loyalty is hard to gain, and for the majority, an extremely hard position to fill. That's why the graves are doubled up now. Trust stands for *true relationships usually stains tragically*. So don't use those two words with me. I'll know when you have passed those highways, partna. But I'ma fuck wit' you one time. And I'ma go along with you because I don't want nobody doing something I wouldn't do myself. But you lucky I ain't kill your lil' dumb ass for approching me with some shit like this.

Nigga, I ain't friendly, but I like your ambition, and I see you motivated on achieving what you done set your mind on.

Stay down and you bound to come up," Maliss said, as they drove down 85 South en route to Sin City.

"Rule number one," Maliss continued, "since you touched on the subject of trust, let me school you on what I look for in a man and woman. Your word should be your bond because if your word is no good, you ain't dependable and you can't be trusted. You should always keep your word no matter what it may cost you. The moment I find out otherwise, we finished, partna, understood?" Maliss asked.

"Ain't no question," Roe Black replied.

"Aight, let me lace you on this lick, cause yo' first one is tonight. There's no more than two niggas in here at the same time. They will be strapped so be on point. Sleepers are in the graveyard. It should be money and dope in there, anywhere from a quick ticket to a half," Maliss said. "Now when we get close to the area, we gone switch cars and get suited up for the situation and wait until the perfect time. It's Memorial Day weekend, everybody tryna get paid, get high, and get fucked. If you have to shoot, do it to win. This game for keeps and I definitely ain't tryna take no dirt nap," Maliss said, and with that, he turned the music up, lit a blunt and rode the rest of the way deep in thought.

Rack it up, Rack it up, Rack it up/ Stack it up, Stack it up, Stack it up

A track by Yo Gotti and Nicki Minaj came through Ayesha's Bose speakers as she swerved streets, pulling up to Swolehead's party. Riding shotgun was her ride or die Santanna.

"Who's that?" Someone yelled as she exited the vehicle.

As Ayesha worked her way through the crowd she heard different voices. "Who da fuck is that?"

"I don't know, but that G-wagon is super clean!"

Ayesha was turning heads in her brand new, pink 63 AMG. Swolehead's party was still packed and it was 1 a.m.

"Girl," Ayesha said, "I'm finna get my mack on big time in this bitch."

"Yeah, until Lil' Wee Wee get here, if he ain't here already," said Santanna.

"Girl, I ain't thinkin' 'bout no damn Lil' Wee Wee. I'm here for Lil' Wayne. I'm finna lick, lick, lick em' like a lolly pop," Ayesha said, sticking her tongue out as if she was in the music video. Everybody stood around, anticipating who was going to exit the G-Wagon.

"No, that ain't who I think it is, is it?" Meeka said.

"Shit, it *shole* look like her, girl," Tee-Tee confirmed.

"Who the fuck invited the tramp of the south?" Meeka asked with much attitude. "Who whip she borrowed?" she added, revealing that her hate was at an all time high.

Ayesha stepped out wearing a black Chanel halter top and a pink mini-skirt by Christan Dior, with a pair of black and pink Jimmy Choo Sandles. Her pink toenail polish and mohawk hairstyle set everything off. She was truly mixing designers but she didn't care.

Santanna on the other hand wore an all black negligee by Louis Vuitton, a pink Louis Vuitton two-piece swimsuit, a pink Louis Vuitton clutch, and black Louis Vuitton flip flops. Her pink toenails and pink dookie braids made her look extra fierce.

"Hey, Swolehead," Ayesha said as she walked right by Meeka and Tee- Tee, giving them the mean-mug.

She reached over and gave Swolehead a hug. "Happy birthday, babe," she said, handing him a two hundred dollar bottle of Smell Like Money cologne by Illegal Activity.

"Good look, babygirl," he said, after he welcomed her embrace.

"Man, this bitch sauced up, hoe," Ayesha said referring to the party. She kept stepping, with Santanna on her heels.

Swolehead put his hand up in front of Santanna, stopping her. She put her hands on her hips and placed her weight on one foot. "What, Swolehead?" she asked.

"Where my gift at, nigga? You all Louis down and shit."

"Oh, here," Santanna reached in to give him a hug.

Swolehead brushed her off. "I'm cool on all that," he told her.

"What? Whateva, nigga. Here," she said and handed him a hundred dollar bill from her purse.

"Now move outta my way 'cause you holdin' me up from gettin' my mack on," she joked, as she bounced her ass up and down to the beat.

"We Luv Dem Girlz" by Small Tyme Ballaz, a local rap group from Montgomery, Alabama, blasted through the speakers as the girls walked toward the backyard.

"Girl look at them Vin Yard Boys over there wit' they ratchet asses, and ain't that Tareyo over there with the Coke Block Boys?" Ayesha asked and pointed.

"Uh huh, yep," Santanna said. "His black ass self. I see the D-Block Boys in this bitch! Girl, they got them Circle-K Boys in this bitch too."

"Oh, okay, if them niggas up in here, we straight then," Ayesha said. Both girls erupted in laughter. "Well come on, we gotta get our drink on and get to vibin' in this bitch."

***

The security buzzer went off as Agent Malone and Agent Patricia entered the door at Universal Spy Shop. "Hey, welcome to Universal Spy Shop. I'm Nick, the assistant. How can I help you today?"

"Well, first we'd like to see the registrations on for all of your tracking devics." Agent Malone held up the necessary affidavits.

Nick nodded and replied, "Okay, that won't be a problem."

"So, who's over the tracking section anyway?" Agent Malone inquired. "Is it you?"

"Oh, no, no, not me," Nick assured him. "As a matter of fact, the guy in charge of that section is off for the next two days, and his name is Donte Williams."

"Okay, can we have a number for this Donte Williams, please?" Agent Malone asked. Saying *please* was his closet attempt at being nice.

"Well, that's classified information, sir. You would have to go through the necessary procedure in order to get that information."

"Okay, we'll come back with a warrant. But, when we do it's not gonna be pretty, Mr. Nick. C'mon, Patricia. let's get outta here," he said, as he turned to walk away.

"Do you think he's covering for him?" Patricia asked, once they were back in the car.

"As of right now, I'm not sure, but time will soon tell," he said. His tone was laced with frustration.

The phone vibrated, signaling an incoming text message to Hawks phone.

Nick: 2 Feds just came by askin bout the demo.

Hawk read it and tapped on his phone's keypad quickly.

Hawk: Damn... bet that up

He pressed send on his phone, then texted Fonzo and told him he needed fifteen more. He told him to hit back within the next 24 hours and he'd have a nice reward for him.

CHAPTER 11

Down the road somewhere in a shed far out in the woods, Lil' Rod held a bucket of muddy pond water. "Wake yo' ass the fuck up fuck boy," he yelled as he threw the mud in BoBo's face. BoBo moaned through the gag as he regained consciousness. He couldn't see but his nostrils were invaded by a strong rancid chemical order.

"So . . . I see you got good taste when it comes to jewelry, huh, nigga?" Lil' Rod reached up and slapped the shit out of BoBo, who was swinging back and forth from a chain, hands tied together overhead on a pole, with his feet shackled together. He picked up the chainsaw that lay at his feet and gave it some extra gas to crank it up louder. BoBo moaned even lounder and pissed his pants.

"Aww, shit, nigga . . . I done literally scared the piss outta you, huh?" Lil' Rod said comically. He lifted the chainsaw up and brushed it across BoBo's chest and bare back. "Now . . . let's talk, and you might regain your life before you lose it, homes."

Lil' Rod reached up and took the blinder off BoBo's face. First thing BoBo noticed was the two big-ass pit bulls in the corner, and a big stainless-steel tub filled with some type of liquid.

"First question: "Did J-Racks put you up to robbing me, or was it your own idea?"

"Mmm-hmm."

"Oh, let me get that for you, my bad." Lil' Rod removed the gag.

"I don't-I don't know what the fuck you talkin' 'bout, nigga."

"Sic 'em!"

Immediately the two pit bulls rushed and attacked BoBo violently, tearing his flesh with their sharp canines.

"Ahhh! Help! Please, get'em , call 'em off! Please!" BoBo yelled at the top of his lungs. Sweat rolled from his face and he didn't care that he was starting to cry like a baby.

"Get right," Lil' Rod commanded. Both dogs stopped and sat down.

"So, you a G, huh? Let me guess . . . you ain't gon' rat yo' boss out, right? Well, fuck-nigga, you shoulda never pulled a gun on me and let me live. You see that tub ova there?" Lil' Rod pointed. "It's filled with sulfuric acid. Yeah, bitch, it will eat through anything except porcelin, stainless-steel, and dirt, partna. Won't be no funeral 'cause ain't nobody gon' find you, and nobody can hear you holla for help. Now . . . I'ma ask you one more time . . . whose idea was it to rob me, his or yours?" BoBo didn't answer fast enough so Lil' Rod ran the chainsaw down his arm slowly.

"Stoooppp . . . Ahhh, shit! Stop man, you fuckin' crazy ass, nigga! I didn't fuckin' ro-ro-rob yo' ass, nigga," BoBo screamed out in agony.

Lil' Rod slapped him across the face, hard. "Stop lying, bitch-ass nigga. How the fuck you get my muthafuckin' chain, pussy!"

BoBo tried to answer as he felt himself about to black out from the shock and loss of blood. "Mm-mm-my man . . . I bought the chain fi-from Lil' Fi-fi-fred," he said before passing out.

"What? What the fuck you say? You fuckin' lying ass nigga? Get yo' bitch ass up!" Lil' Rod slapped him even harder and BoBo lifted his head. "I'ma ask you again, where you get this from, nigga. I ain't bullshittin'." He cranked the chainsaw again and held it as close as he could to BoBo's face without slicing it in half.

"Nigga, Lil' Fred sold it to me yesterday for fifteen bands, on my grandmama, no lie!" BoBo yelled with all the energy he had. Lil' Rod swung the chainsaw with one swift stroke and BoBo's head hit the floor and rolled.

"Oh, yeah, this my pussy ain't it," Lil' Wee Wee said to Ayesha.

"Yesss!"

"Who pussy is this?" he demanded.

"Yourrss!" She lied.

"Damn. Right. It. Is," he said, pounding with every word, as he continued to grudge-fuck her with all his might. He had her in the doggie-style, in the back seat of his Hell Cat Charger, in the parking lot outside of Swolehead's party.

"Turn over." He flipped her in submission style. "Mmm, got damn this pussy good! I'm finna put a baby in you."

"Noo, you betta not nut in me, Lenard!"

"Ahh, shit, girl . . . I couldn't help it."

"What? Get the fuck off me stupid. This our last time since you can't seem to *help* it," she said, rolling from up underneath him to get dressed.

Lil' Wee Wee was breathing hard but didn't care, he had gotten his. Now he sat naked as his phone vibrated back-to-back with texts messages. He looked at the screen and saw it had been Meeka blowing his shit up for the last fifteen minutes straight.

"Where the fuck this midget at? I been texting and calling and he ain't answering. I'ma slap the shit outta his ass if I find out he playin' a bitch," Meeka told Tee-Tee. "All of a sudden that tramp and him missin' at the same time.

Shake whatcha mama gave ya / shake
whatcha mama gave ya / clap clap clap
clap . . .

When Ayesha walked back through the fence of the back-yard, Santanna was on stage with her hands on her knees, making it clap and going hard for the booty shaking contest

"There go that hoe right there," Meeka said aloud, but she wouldn't dare approach her. Meeka knew she was no match for Ayesha, but she would try Lil' Wee Wee since he was only four feet eleven inches tall.

"There that bitch go right there, boy," Dirt Bag said. "Everything in place, right?" he asked Lil' Suwoo.

"Yeah, Blood. She all hooked up, partna. We gonna get her ass tonight and make her take us to that nigga Maliss and then rob and whack they asses. Fuck wrong wit' them!" Lil' Suwoo said.

"Alright, it's just a matter of time," Lil' Wee Wee agreed.

"Alright, everybody, it's been fun but there's been a slight change of plans," Swolehead said over the mic. "I know y'all ready to see Lil' Wayne and the Migos, right?"

"Yeahhhh," the whole crowd yelled.

"Well, I just received a call from Weezy himself apologizing because he can't make it here." Everyone in the audience booed, and Swolehead knew he had to do something before they stormed the place and tore everything up.

"Hold up, now, I ain't finished yet. He said he sorry they couldn't make it 'cause he know everybody was all hyped to see them. But if you wanna see him and the Migos, they wit' 1st Degree on his Black Lives Matter tour. They gonna be performing tonight at Club Gwopped Up, off Atlanta Highway.

Plus, I'm havin' the money fight there anyway, so if yo' money real long and strong then bring it on. The first one hundred fifty ladies get in free on me, and drinks free all night. So y'all better fuck something, while y'all bullshittin'," he yelled to the crowd.

"Ain't you glad you came down, girl!" Santanna said to Ayesha.

"Yeah, bitch. It's been a minute since I hung out like this, for real."

CHAPTER 12

Friday night, May 26, 2020: Sin City

"BoBo ain't answered his phone in a minute," Red Dog said to J-Racks. "Fuck he got goin' on. He was 'sposed to re-up today and shit, that's what I'm talkin' bout . . . can't depend on these young niggas for shit these days," J-Racks said.

"Well, I sent Man-Man and them through the View to locate the nigga and they said a female named Falesha said somebody jumped out wit' a mask on and pistol whipped him. She took off for her life and didn't look back, but whoever it did it was drivin' a black two-door car."

"What kind of car?" J-Racks asked.

"She didn't know, but said it looked like one of them fast cars," Red Dog said.

"Damn, that ain't tellin' me shit," J-Racks replied.

Meanwhile, on the southside of Sin City, Lil' Fred was feeling himself. Shit he'd made fifteen grand off the chain and he'd managed to talk Monkey Wrench Joe into paying him fifteen more for the truck. He went and bought him a Rolex with the cash.

"This bitch on sumin'. I'm wearing this to club Big City Sunday when 1st Degree get here on his Black Lives Matter tour. I'ma be pullin' up in a drop-top rari on they asses, nigga! This my city and I can't wait till these lames see this shit. I'm finna fuck the city up!" he said out loud. "Yeah, I can't lose. *And* I heard somebody snatched that bitch-ass nigga BoBo up," Lil' Fred said. He just might be dead. Damn, my luck couldn't get no better."

"What up, boy," he said, hugging a bottle of Patron when Lil' Rod entered the house.

"Ain't shit, partna. What's up wit' you?" Lil' Rod asked.

"Ain't too much my nigga, had to go get the Rollie on 'em. Gettin' ready for the Black Lives Matter concert on Sunday. Shit, you better get yo' shit right too, nigga 'cause I'm finna shit on 'em this time," Lil' Fred said, smirking to himself seeing Lil' Rod chainless. "What's in the bag?" he asked.

"Oh, I stopped by Lowes and picked up some house supplies, homes. Something light. I'll be right back. Shit, pour me a cup of that 'trons, nigga. Let me drink wit' you."

Lil' Rod left and went to the bathroom. "Got his bitch ass," he said to himself. He opened the medicine cabinet and closed it back, making noises as if he was putting shit up. Then he opened the cabinet underneath the sink and slammed it closed, causing something to fall. When he reopened the cabinet, he saw a small wallet with a picture of Sky inside it.

"Muthafuckin', bitch-ass, double-crossin' ass, pussy nigga." He spoke low but his anger boiled inside him. He put the chain on that had been inside the bag, then put on a pair of black leather gloves. He flushed the toilet and put Sky's wallet in his back pocket before grabbing the chicken wire out of the bag.

He eased up behind Lil' Fred and dropped the wallet in his lap, while simultaneously wrapping the chicken wire around his neck with lightning speed. Lil' Fred began choking immediately.

"Pussy-ass nigga! How you gonna do me like that after all we been through," Lil' Rod said, pulling on the wire with all his might. Lil' Fred struggled for air and kicked over the coffee table, going wild with panic.

Suddenly, with a loud crack, the door flew open and off the hinges. "Put your muthafuckin' hands up, bitch-ass niggas!"

Lil' Rod continued to pull, thinking to himself that Lil' Fred had some how called the rescue team. But, either way, he was determined to finish what he'd started.

"I said, put your hands up before I swiss cheese your bitch ass!" Roe Black said.

Slowly, Lil' Rod released Lil' Fred and put his hands up. Lil' Fred coughed up blood and spit while grabbing his neck. Roe Black went over and smacked Lil' Fred with the pistol. "I said, put your hands up, nigga." This time, Lil' Fred managed to raise his shaking hands.

"We gonna be real fast, so y'all can finish y'all little dispute," Maliss said through the voice scrambler disguising his voice. "So . . . by now, y'all already know what we here for, right? If not, we here for it all, my niggas, startin' with the case. Oh, and if you play, then it's definitely a dirt nap, partnas."

"Where its at?" Roe Black questioned the duo.

"Where *what* at, bruh?" Lil' Rod asked. His face twisted from anger as if his looks alone would be enough to kill Roe Black.

"Oh, my bad, you didn't know I had it, did you . . . you lookin' for this, nigga?" Roe Black smacked the FN against Lil' Rod's head until he fell. "Pussy nigga," he said and struck him again. "Where that gwap at, partna?"

Maliss pointed his Draco at Lil' Fred's head. "Don't shoot, you shoulda asked me first. Fuck that shit, we can get that shit back but you only get one life," Lil' Fred said.

"That's right, I see you the smartest," Maliss laughed.

"This ain't my shit, anyway, fuck all that. I'm just a distributor, homes. Fuck this nigga and fuck this shit, too. After this I'm through wit' this shit anyway. I don't give a fuck," Lil' Fred said.

"Man, shut yo' hoe ass up, nigga, and take us to the money!" Roe Black said.

"You pussy muthafucka, I'ma kill yo' bitch-ass if they don't kill us first, rat-ass nigga," Lil' Rod said, trying to get up.

A swift kick from Maliss in the ribs sent him back down. "Who told you to get yo' ass up, nigga? Don't fuckin' move unless I say move! Yo, Black, walk Lil' Fred back to the safe," he told his partna in crime. "Nice and easy, partna. If you move too swift I'ma park yo' ass for good, understood?"

"Yeah, I understand. I got you. I ain't gonna play wit' my life," Lil' Fred fired back.

All of sudden, Maliss brought the pistol down on his head. "Shut the fuck up! What you tryna do, distract me or something, nigga?"

"Nah, man, I got you, okay," Lil' Fred whimpered.

"Look, I'ma let you kill yo' boy since he folded so easily. I hate weak niggas, partna. Plus, it looked like that's what you was finna do anyway before we came and interrupted you," Maliss told Lil' Rod.

"Get yo' hoe ass over there and sit down," Roe Black said, once he'd emptied the safe. He shoved Lil' Fred down on the love seat.

"Was that everything?" Maliss asked Black.

"Yeah, from what I could tell. Hold up, let's ask pie man over there," Roe Black said. "Was that everything, pussy boy?" he asked Lil' Fred.

"Yeah, man. I gave you everything that was here, on God!" he said.

"Nah, you lying. I can tell," Roe Black said.

"No I ain't, man! That's on God," Lil' Fred cried out.

"Nigga, who you think I am? Do you think I believe you? Believe in God? And while we at it, take that Rollie off, fuck boy." Roe Black pointed his FN at him.

Lil' Fred hesitated for a second, never noticing Maliss slip Lil' Rod an eight-inch double bladed army knife, nor did Roe Black see it.

"Alright, that's everything," Black said. He looked at Lil' Rod's chain and decided, "I'ma let you keep that this time, nigga."

"Alright, you know what to do," Maliss said to Lil' Rod. Lil' Rod rushed Lil' Fred before he ever had time to react, stabbing him multiple times in the neck.

Lil' Fred had a little fight left in him but only enough to put his hands to his throat for one last attempt at survival. He tried to scream but the words were clotted by his own blood.

Lil' Rod then hit Lil' Fred in the stomach repeatedly, cutting large gashes in his flesh and exposing the raw internal organs. As gangsta as he was, Roe Black winced at the gruesome, horrific sight.

"Come on," Maliss said once he was satisfied, "Let's go."

"Pussy-ass nigga, fuck yo' bitch-ass, weak ass! I got something for yo' ass, nigga. Fuck you!"

Lil' Fred was long dead yet Lil' Rod continued to stab him relentlessly. He had turned into mad man with a lust for spilled blood and couldn't contain himself. "Robbed a nigga then got my ass robbed!" Maliss and Roe Black left as Lil' Rod was cutting away at Lil' Fred's mutilated body.

CHAPTER 13

I be ridin' round town / waitin' for da' lick to go down / Goin' Fed with that yappa / keep a hundred plus rounds / travelin' hard wit' that work tryin' my best to stay in bounds / ain't no tellin' when I rob/ get on da floor, don't make a sound / I be ridin' round town / ridin' ridin' round town

"That nigga 1st Degree got heat, don't he, girl!" Santanna said.

"Yeah, he definitely on something," Ayesha said, feeling tipsy from the Cristal they had been sipping on in the VIP section.

"Aight, ya'll know what time it is, but first we'd like to give another round of applause for my main man 1st Degree. And he got another song for us before he depart, so stay ready," DJ I-Got-That-Heat said.

"I'ma pass it over to the man of the night, Swolehead!"

"Is the westside in this bitch?" Swolehead asked.

"You know it!" the crowd returned.

"Southside, where you at?" he screamed.

"Southhhh Sideeee," the crowd replied.

"Northside, make some noise!"

"The best side!" they sang out.

"What about that east?" Swolehead asked.

"Gwaped up!" the crowd yelled.

"That's right, I hear y'all. Alright, now, whose money the longest?"

"Ahh!" The crowd went wild.

"Okay, now, let's get this shit started then. Each side will have a chance to throw money until the chorus of the song ends then it'll be swept up in a pile and counted. Whoever has the most, wins. All the money will be split between everybody from that side and they get a free Money Fight T-shirt and hat, and their picture in the Money Fight Hall of Fame!" Swolehead yelled into the mic.

"Alright, everybody section off with your side. We gonna start wit' the westside first, then the south, then the north, and last is the east. May the best side win!"

I got plenty money / what's in my pocket dog / big face hundreds. Money went flying in the air as Plies' song came on.

"This my favorite part right here," Dirt Bag said to Suwhoop.

"Damn right. Victim time," Suwhoop said. "Thanks, Swolehead, you help us find a sucka every week. boy."

"Hell yeah, my nigga, you know what to say. Now, pick us a few vics and then we'll rap and trap ol' girl," Dirt Bag said.

"Okay, now that we have the proper amounts for each side and there's only one winner. So if you didn't win, you better get yo' hussle on, parnta. So first, we got that dirty westside, totaling at two thousand eight hundred dollars. Next, you got that mighty southside, totaling at two thousand seven hundred sixty-eight dollars," Swolehead said, as the crowd applauded and booed at the same time. "Next, we got that nitty gritty northside, totaling at three thousand four hundred forty-six dollars."

"Northside, northside!" the north yelled out from the crowd.

"Aight, y'all hold up 'cause it ain't over yet. Now, last but not least, we got that wealthy eastside coming in and winning the Money Fight by a landslide!" Swolehead said. "That's a total of nine thousand fifteen dollars to be split between y'all and y'all also win Money Fight T-shirts and hats. Now, y'all need to head to to the picture booth to take y'all Hall of Fame pictures."

"Eastside! Eastside!" The eastside members of the crowd went wild with excitement from the acknowledgement of the win.

"Shit, Blood, we gotta slide over on that eastside sometime this week, my nigga. I already know Phat-Phat chewin' good," Suwhoop said to Dirt Bag.

"Yeah, I got something for that ass. You already know, but right now I got my eye on the prize, homes," Dirt Bag said, watching Ayesha and Santanna like a hawk.

"Oh yeah, Monkey Town!" 1st Degree screamed, making his way to the stage.

"Yeah," the crowd yelled back.

"I just want y'all to hear it firsthand from the horse's mouth . . . all my lyrics and rhymes tell a story about my past. It might be where I'm from but it ain't where I'm at or where I'm going, feel me?

See, I fucks wit this city 'cause it's a city that came from the struggle and y'all stand for something. It's a black city, and when we stick together as blacks, we make super boss moves, feel me? They don't like it when we become aware of life, in general. Once you realize your power and start applyin' it, that's when the accidental police killings start. They want to kill us off and they call themselves doin' it with the drugs, prisons, guns, which all comes from them. But I ain't gonna burn y'all ears wit' the positive talk but do know I care 'bout my black folks. I know y'all been drinkin' good in this bitch, and I hope y'all have had a good time, just know that 12 is out there waitin' on y'all so they can pass out DUIs, drugs, and guns. So if you do get pulled over tonight, ask 'em:

"Who is they / I don't know 'em / I don't trust 'em/ I don't wanna / try da take me / I ain't goin' / I ain't lyin' /
I'ma buss 'em / Fuck da law / Fuck da law, y'all / Fuck da law / Fuck da law y'all / I'ma rob if I wanna, sell drugs if I wanna / Pop pills when I wanna, big heavy marjuanna /

111

Fuck da law / Fuck da law, y'all!"

The crowd went crazy and everyone rapped along with the lyrics. When 1st Degree finished his set, surprise guests, Ice Cold, Present, and Yanca graced the stage and bursted out with:

"I keep da choppa an da seat / so I'ma hundred niggas deep / Feds wanna take my life / don't want a real nigga free / PO can't control me / fuck nigga don't know me/ I ain't been in a prison yet that can muthafuckin' hold me!"

CHAPTER 14

"Gone out there, Blood. I'm finna take a piss before I light the city up, Blood," Dirt Bag said.

"Yeah, hurry yo' ass up, nigga. Let me find out yo' nerves ain't shit," Suwhoop laughed.

"Yeah, haha hell. Get yo' ass out to the car, nigga," Dirt Bag said, as he left en route to the bathroom.

"There it is, partna, twenty-two thousand five hundred. Paid in full, my nigga. You put on for the city, homes."

"Oh shit," Dirt Bag said, overhearing Swolehead counting money out to 1st Degree.

"Right on time, hell yeah. Gotta make something shake just as soon as I take a leak," 1st Degree told Swolehead.

"Alright, partna, y'all be safe on that road," Swolehead said.

"Bet that up, bruh. Stay up, we'll see each other again."

"C'mon, bruh. Let's put this play in motion real fast before we go," Dirt Bag said.

"Fa' sho'. What da lick read?" Suwhoop said, exiting the car. He cluthed his weapon, ready for whatever as they quietly rounded the Y en route to the tour bus.

"Yo' Degree," Dirt Bag hollered.

"What's up? 1st Degree said, as he turned around and faced Dirt Bag.

"Man, before y'all get outta here, I need you to autograph this CD for me real fast, bruh. My lil' sister gon' kill me if I come home without it," Dirt Bag explained as he stalled the rapper. Everyone else kept walking to the bus. He handed him the CD,

"You got a pen, Man?" 1st Degree asked.

"Yeah, my bad, it's right here, partna," Dirt Bag said and came up with a 30 round GLOCK 40.

"Put yo' muthafuckin' hands up, stupid ass nigga . . . you know what it is!"

"What the fuck," 1st Degree shouted.

"Yeah, drop that bag, bitch-ass nigga," Suwhoop said, pointing his pistol too.

Although the crowd had already boarded the bus and closed the door, a spectator had been watching through the window of the bus as they robbed 1st Degree, and called the police.

"Take all that shit off, nigga, and hurry the fuck up before I shoot yo' lame ass, pussy," Dirt Bag said. "That was a good lil' speech in there, all that *black lives matter* shit. Nigga, you gonna go a long way, homes. But this is Monkey Town-Murda Town, nigga. Cut-throat! Don't *no* lives matter out here, fuck-nigga! 'Preciate the donation, and don't forget to sign my CD." Dirt Bag shoved the CD in 1st Degrees' hand and waited until he scribbled his name before snatching it back and running off, laughing.

"Damn, man, these bitch-ass niggas got me," 1st Degree said out loud.

"C'mon, c'mon, are you okay?" Yanca asked, coming off the bus, running.

"Hell, fuck nah I ain't okay. These niggas just worked me over. That nigga Swellhead probably done set me up," 1st Degree said, mad as hell.

"It's *Swoleheud*," Ice Cold said from the bus window.

"What? Man, fuck you and fuck that nigga. I don't give a fuck what his name is! I ain't neva comin' back down here no mo'. Broke ass niggas." He continued to fuss as he climbed onto the bus.

"Hell yeah, that's what I'm talkin' 'bout. Anybody can get it. Fuck these niggas, Blood," Suwhoop said to Dirt Bag as they drove off.

"Yeah, that shit was nothin'. Now hurry up and get us to Krystal's. They should still be in line since we wasn't gone that long," Dirt Bag said

"Yeah, yeah, yeah, I'm on it, bruh."

"Welcome to Krystal's, how may I take your order?" the cashier asked politely.

"Can I get a number 5 with no onions, and make them fries chili cheese, and a super-size Hi-C, please. And hold on, I got a second order," Ayesha said.

"Okay, order when ready," the cashier said through the speaker box of the drive-thru lane.

"What you want, bitch?" Ayesha asked Santanna. Santanna leaned over from the passenger side, "Um, yeah, get me a number 3 with extra pickles, chili cheese fries, and a super-size Hi-C," she yelled out the window.

The cashier read back the orders and said, "Okay, that'll be $7.89 for the first order and $6.52 for the second. Will that be all?"

"Yes," Ayesha acknowledged.

"Okay, drive around, please. Thank you."

"There go them hoes right there. Pull around and get behind them when they pull out," Dirt Bag said. "Matter-of-fact, fuck that, let me out right here. It's show time, nigga. The door might be unlocked so I'm finna jump down on 'em. Don't let 'em get out the parkin' lot."

"Bet that," Suwhoop said.

"Thank you for shopping at Krystal's. Come again," the cashier said. Ayesha received their meals, smiled, and let the window up.

A sharp tap on Santanna's window startled her off guard. "Who the fuck is that?" she said.

"Let me holla at you for a second," Dirt Bag said through the window.

"Don't roll my window down," Santanna said, feeling funny about the whole ordeal. Ayesha cracked it slightly. "What," she yelled, with her usual sassy attitiude.

"Damn. boo. I'm just tryna holla at you real quick."

"We good," Ayesha said. She rolled the window back up and tried to pull off, quickly.

Dirt Bag tried to snatch the door open but it was locked. He drew his strap from his waist. "Get the fuck outta the truck, bitch!" he ordered. Both girls screamed and Ayesha hit the gas, swerving out of control and was suddenly cut off by a black '89 Trans Am.

"Get the fuck outta the damn truck," Suwhoop said, just as Dirt Bag caught back up to the vehicle. He hit the window with the pistol, trying to break the glass but it bounced off.

"Hell nah, get the fuck away from my truck, bitch," Ayesha screamed, "I'm callin' the police right now!"

Dirt Bag stepped back and let off three shots.

She hit the gas pedal of the V12 and rammed right through the Trans Am.

"Fuck! C'mon, c'mon, c'mon, get in, Blood," Suwhoop said to Dirt Bag. He climbed in as Suwhoop swerved the car out of the parking lot, chasing behind the pink G-Wagon,

"I'm finna kill these bitches, bruh! Hurry up and catch up wit' 'em real fast," Dirt Bag said. His adrenaline was on ten and he was getting more hyper and anxious by the second.

"Shit, shit, shit!" Ayesha cried, still in shock—more than anything, she was glad the windows were bulletproof. "Yes, we on South Blvd right now . . . Yes, they chasin' us right now, ma'am," Santanna answered; the police dispatcher was on the other end of the call.

"Fuck, Blood. We ain't gonna catch up wit' 'em, bruh. That bitch runnin' that truck," Suwhoop said. The truck was too fast for the Trans Am and he was losing speed on the chase.

Ayesha pushed the vehicle with everything it had, not realizing Maliss had installed a chip in the engine to boost its power. She attempted to call him but to no avail. She had already called twice, and it had gone straight to voicemail, on her third try she began to cry.

"Umm, yes, we are on South Blvd, at the light, about to turn on Mobile Highway," Santanna informed the dispatcher. Just as she'd gotten the last word out, a hard impact caused her to drop the phone.

Suwoop had run the Trans Am right into the back of the truck. He quickly put it in reverse and rammed it again as Dirt Bag shot off three more rounds into the body of the G-Wagon. Even though the Trans Am was taking most of the impact, Suwhoop backed up again and smashed into them even harder.

"Fuck this shit!" Ayesha threw her truck in reverse, burning the pavement. At the same time Suwhoop propelled forward, Ayesha repelled backward. Instantly, they collided with a loud bang only causing damage to the front-end of the Trans.

Ayesha regained control and sped through the light.

"Fuck, fuck, fuck! Where the fuck are the police," Santanna cried into the phone. Ayesha banged on the steering wheel from both, fear and anger.

"Hold on, ma'am. We have a car almost to your location," the dispatcher said.

"Fuck, we'll catch them hoes on the back fade, Blood. Get us outta here before 12 get on this shit. Hell, we did good for a night's work," Dirt Bag said as Suwhoop wheeled the busted vehicle off the street.

"Damn bitch-ass niggas done fucked my truck up and I just got my shit. Now I'ma have to explain this shit to Maliss."

Ayesha and Santanna had just given their reports of the incident to the police and they were leaving the station. "You okay?" she asked Santanna.

"I'm a little shook up, but I'll come around. Just get me home. I need some damn sleep."

"I think you need to come back to the A with me for a few weeks until this shit cool down. We don't even know what really happened. Plus, we got plenty of room for you, and Gabby and Maya can catch up on playin' with each other."

"I'm game." Santanna replied without a second thought.

***

Back on D-Block, Dirt Bag and Suwhoop was chillin' at the hangout. "That's eleven thousand two hundred fifty dollars straight down the middle, Blood," Dirt Bag said and laughed. He was feeling good after the lick they'd made.

"Check this bitch-ass nigga out, man . . . I shoulda shot that bitch with all that custom-ass, fake-ass jewelry, bruh. Nigga out here flauntin' and shit, bout to get killed over some shit that ain't even legit. We still gonna finness these niggas out here in the streets. Thay ain't gonna know the difference, watch that I tell you, Blood."

"I'm already hip," Suwhoop said. They gonna get it just 'cause it's 1st Degree shit. We got a AP, Cuban link bracelet and matchin' chain, and two pinky rings. We should be able to make at least seventy-five bands out these niggas."

"Yeah, streets talk so let me be the first to expose it. This that lame ass nigga 1st Degree shit right here. Yeah, real spit homies, this Murda Town and you know we rock-a-bitch to sleep. Made that pussy nigga get naked and ride out the city wit' his ass out." Dirt Bag laughed at his own humor.

"Now you can buy your shit back 'cause Black lives matter and this shit up for grabs, first come, first serve. Seventy-five racks and this shit gone. Savage life nigga," Dirt Bag said as he smiled into his iPhone camera. "Gone 'head and load that shit up, Blood."

Suwhoop did as he was told and uploaded the video to Instagram, Snapchat, Facebook, and WorldStarHipHop. It went viral, instantly.

"Aww, man, look at these pussy ass niggas tryna tarnish a nigga's name, man. Damn. This shit ain't a good look," 1st Degree said. After seeing the video he immdeiately went in the studio and recorded a diss song.

"Yeah, I'm on highway 78 now. I'll be there in seven minutes," Fonzo said into the phone,

"Aight, bet. I'm in the black long sleeve backed in with the thirty-four forgies, can't miss it," Hawk said, "and hurry yo' ass up, boy. You makin' me miss all that good pussy in there. I just saw Deanna fall in that bitch, too. You already know I'm goin' in that bitch for a few," he said.

Fonzo laughed. "I'm on the way, double-time, player. I'm 'bout to fall up in there."

"Aight, man, see you when you get here. Now get off my phone so I can look at these hoes. Oh yeah, it's on highway 78, Brocket Road. All these bitches up in here made me forget the directions," Hawk said, standing outside Strokes, a popular strip club in Atlanta Georgia.

Maliss climbed in the back seat and laid on the floor. Hawk adjusted the music to the right volume. "Somebody tried to snatch my bitch up in Y-Town, bruh."

"Oh yeah, I'm already on it. I got a reward out for some info, and I'ma find out the details after we handle this, bruh. But pause that, Fonze just pulled up. It's show time," Hawk said.

Maliss remained on the floor with his gloves on, and Fonzo hopped inside the truck. He had a piece of chicken wire wrapped around his hands, waiting for the right moment.

There was a tracker on ol' boy's truck and now the Feds were on it, looking for Fonzo everywhere. *Fuck it,* Maliss thought to himself. He had long come to realize that in this game, anyone was expendable, except him. . . . Unless a nigga showed him otherwise.

"I got 150 percs like you asked for, my nigga. So did you hold your end?" Hawk asked him as soon as his butt hit the seat.

"Yeah, but this gonna have to be that last time for a while, bruh, 'cause I heard the Feds wanna question me 'bout some trackers that came up in a murder or some shit," Fonzo said.

"So what you gonna tell 'em, 'cause they definitely not gonna leave it alone."

"Shit, man, I'ma tell 'em I don't remember nothin'. I'ma tell 'em I didn't have shit to do wit' sellin' no trackers off record."

"I don't know, Fonzo," Hawk contemplated, "that don't sound like a good enough excuse, homes. These are the fuckin' Feds, bruh."

"I know, but what else can I come up with, then?" Fonzo asked.

"You just have to calm down and think. It'll come to you. But, hey, where the percs at?" Hawk asked.

"Yeah, I hope so. But alright, just let me pop three of these to help me relax, bruh. Here they are, all ten like you requested. But, like I said, make sure they last 'cause it's gonna be a while before I— Fonzo' words were cut short and replaced by the sounds of him choking and gagging.

"Go to sleep, nigga. Go to sleep 'cause you shoulda had yo' shit together." Maliss pulled the chicken wire with all his strength, trying to saw off Fonzo's head.

"Sorry, homie but it's all about business, and in this game, security is first, feel me?" Hawk said from the driver's seat while patting on Fonzo's knee.

Fonzo's eyes bulged from his skull as he released all the food he'd eaten that week. He gasped and strained for air until his struggle for life ended.

When the coast was clear, Maliss and Hawk exited the truck and got into a black Maximum and eased out of the parking lot as if nothing had happened.

The truck had been on the police's radar, compliments of Roe Black who turned out to be a great asset to Maliss. However, he never bothered to tell Hawk about the young solder, but instead, chose to keep it to himself in case he needed an ace in the hole. He understood the fine points of the game very well, meaning, never let your left hand know what your right is doing, and keep your cards close to your chest so no one could see the hand you were playing.

***

"Damn, it's extra nice out here in Douglasville, bitch," Santanna said, looking at all the expensive houses in the quiet suburban neighborhood. "Hell yeah, girl, you livin' the flyy life compared to where we come from. Look at this damn crib, bitch. This look like one of them celebrity houses. How many square feet is this anyway?" she wondered aloud.

"15,000," Ayesha said.

"Good God, you need a hoverboard to get across this muthafucka," Santanna said as they pulled up to the Ayesha's estate.

"Fuck all that clit ridin', bitch. C'mon, let's get in the pool and have some drinks. Shit, you know you good wit' me," Ayesha told her.

"Nah, bitch, ain't nobody clit ridin', boo. I'm just sayin', I didn't know it was gonna be like this." Santanna was amazed at how her friend was living and she was happy to be there.

Well you shoulda known 'cause I got that straight drop, have a nigga straight addicted, comin' back geekin' and shit," Ayesha said, pointing down toward her pussy.

"Shit, you ain't got no fiya like that down there, bitch." Santana laughed as they went to change into their swimsuits.

"Shit, you got me fucked up! My shit slippery when wet," Ayesha remarked with pride.

"Bitch, that's TMI," Santanna said using the acronym for 'to much information'. That lil' wet-wet you claim you got ain't gonna help me none, hoe," she laughed.

"Yeah, you can't get none of this but I can show you how to catch a real nigga, bitch. Wrap and trap a nigga, slippery pussy, pussy-whip. pussy strength, pussy power, bitch!" Ayesha shouted out humorously.

"You ain't gotta tell me, bitch. 'Tanna keep a bitch nigga wrapped and trapped. Cheers to the power of the P," they said in unison. Ayesha grabbed her portable security monitor so she could keep an eye on the kids while she and Santanna relaxed in the pool.

"What's that?" Santanna asked.

"A security system. I can see, talk, and hear everything around this bitch," Ayesha said, playing with the controls of the remote device.

"Oh, that's what's up."

"What you drinkin' on, girl?" Ayesha asked from the bar in the middle of the infinity pool.

"Let me get a glass of Ace, please."

122

"Okay, that'll be $35 a flute, bitch," Ayesha joked. She giggled as she made the drink then handed it to Santanna.

"That's fine, just swipe my credit card down the crack of your ass, hoe!" The women erupted with laughter.

"Damn, I'm glad we okay, for real. Them lame ass niggas tried a bitch, but they betta be glad I ain't have my baby with me or I woulda blasted they ass." Ayesha held up a plastic GLOCK 9 pistol.

"Oh, shit. girl. That bitch as pretty as Shocka Zulu's dick. Let me see it." Santanna reached for the weapon like a kid on Christmas day.

"My bae bought it for my birthday last year. It was cotton candy pink you would've though it was a toy. It even shoot underwater, and it's ninety-seven percent acurate. Shout out to the dude Gaston Glock," said Ayesha, paying homage to the Austrian creator of the world's first plastic handgun.

"This shit is light-weight," Santanna said. "I can handle one of these," she added, as she held the gun with two hands. Some how, she lost her grip and it fell. When it landed in the bottom of the pool, it accidently discharged, causing a big splash. "Oops, my bad."

"Shit, girl. Now, my neighbors might call the police, crazy ass bitch. Ayesha looked around to make sure none of the neighbors had come outside.

"I'm sorry, I didn't mean to. Why didn't you tell. it was loaded?"

"Fuck all that. Why the hell you pull the trigger anyway?" Ayesha snapped.

"You know a bitch trigger happy," Santanna replied, making light of the situation. Ayesha checked the monitors and saw the girls were still playing. Just as she thought no one had paid attention to gun being fired, she looked up and noticed the police. "Oh, shit, they already here."

"Who already here?" Santanna asked in a worried tone.

"12 bitch." Ayesha climbed out of the pool and wrapped a towel around her body and then threw on a light robe.

"Damn, that was fast," Santanna said, getting out of the pool behind her.

"Yeah, that's how you know you in the white folks neighborhood." Ayesha stepped to the speaker that communicated to the front gate. "Just a minute," she said to the officer whose face appeared on the screen of the monitor.'

"How are doing today, ma'am?" the officer asked. "I'm here because we received a call in regard to gunshots being fired from this area. We wanted to make sure everything is okay around here," the officer informed her. "If wouldn't mind coming out to answer some questions, that would be helpful."

"No problem. I'll let you through the gate and meet you in the front. She walked through the house and opened the door still wrapped in the towel and robe. The male officer took a slow look at her body from head to toe, then glanced behind her, trying to get a better look inside the house.

"Everything is fine, sir. I was in the backyard getting ready to clean my pistol and my finger accidently tapped the trigger before I could unload it. It's my fault."

"Oh, okay. That's not a problem. Do you have a license to carry, ma'am?"

"Yes, I do," Ayesha said, slightly annoyed at having to go through so many questions for nothing.

"Do you mind if I see them, please. If everything check out, I'll be on my way." He smiled, politely.

"Well, yes you can, but you'll have to pull it up on your computer. I'm not about to go all the way back in there and come all the way back. This is a very big home, sir," Ayesha said, adding the intended sass in her words.

"Yes, I understand. Just give me your info," he said.

She complied and five minutes later he said, "You're good to go, and you've been verified, ma'am. Thank you for your time, and please be more careful. I would hate for you to shoot yourself or someone else by accident. You know those things do happen."

"Yes, I understand, and thank you for your concern and for responding to the call so quickly, sir. But, I'm well qualified when it comes to using a weapon," Ayesha assured.

The officer nodded. "But mistakes can and do happen. Goodnight, ma'am," he said, as he turned to leave.

Ayesha closed the door. *Dumb ass Santanna*, she thought on her way back to the pool .

"What he say?" Santanna asked.

"He said he could smell the Fendi perfume from my pussy and wanted to test it to see if it tastes just as sweet as it smelled, bitch," Ayesha said.

Santanna laughed hysterically. "Bitch, you stupid as hell."

"But, for real tho', he said to be more careful when I clean the gun or somebody could get shot. Luckily I hadn't started drinking yet, otherwise he would've smelled the alcohol on my breath." She poured herself drink.

"So, yeah, like I was sayin', 'cause of the incident that happened at the drive-thru the other night, Maleek call hisself investigatin' a bitch, feel me? Interrogatin' me and shit 'cause I was 'sposed to been visitin' my family *not* goin' to no damn party. Now it look suspect and shit, and he mad as hell 'bout the situation. He even had the nerve to take the keys to my new truck."

While Ayesha spoke, Santanna was on her phone texting.

Santanna: Im in the A wit Ayesha. She hit send and sent the message to Lil' Wee-Wee.

"Well, he'll he fine," Santanna said. Ayesha checked her monitors and the girls had fallen asleep.

"Yeah, I guess so," she said. "Fuck it, 'cause it is what it is. Now come on, let's go take a shower then find us something to eat," Ayeshe. said.

"You. can use the bathroom in the guest room. Come on. Let me show you where everything is." She pulled the closet open. "I'll bring you a bar of my cosmetic black soap and all that shit. Matter-of-fact, I'll be right back. Let me gone get that that now."

The bathroom was laid in earth tone, brown marble, heated floors. The counter was brown and trimmed in gold, and there was a gold sink, and brown seat. The body temperture shower adjusted the water to your body temperture.

"Damn, this bitch is laid and four times bigger than my bedroom," Santanna said astonished. At the same time she marveled over the luxurious bathroom, a text came through on her phone:

Lil' Wee Wee: Where you at hoe?
Why? she texted back.

"Okay, here you go. Let me know if you need anything else," Ayesha said. "I'm about to go freshen up myself."

"Alright, thanks, girl," Santanna told her.

"Stop playin', you know you my sis, and it's always family over everything so I got you, bitch," Ayesha said sincerely.

"That's real." Santanna said back, but Ayesha had already walked away and hadn't heard her. She felt bad for not telling her about her and Lil' Wee Wee. In her mind, he was just Ayesha's side-piece so her relationship with him wasn't really violating—at least, not to her.

Damn, I done fucked around and left the damn monitor outside. The girls probably still sleep though, Ayesha thought, as rinsed the soap off her naked body. Once she was done showering, she stepped out to dry off but left the water running. *I better hurry my ass up so I can check on them kids 'cause ain't no tellin' if Santanna gonna do it wit' her forgetful self.*

She reached in and turned the water off and turned the light off in the bathroom. As she made her way down the hallway, she thought she heard talking and figured the girls were up. However, the closer she got to the voice, the clearer it became where the voice was actually coming from.

"Oh, shit, yes . . . give me that big ol' dickm baby. You know you been wantin' some of this," the familiar voice said lustfully.

"What the fuck?" Ayeslia said aloud. Her blood began to boil and she could feel her body as it began to shake from rage. She ran back to the bathroom and grabbed the pink GLOCK she had left lying on the counter. Hurriedly, she did a 360 back down the hall.

"You love this pussy, don't you? You want all this pussy, don't you, Maliss?" Santanna said provacatively. "Umm, yes, baby, fuck this pussy good, boy . . . Oh my God . . . ooh I'm 'bout to cum all over this dick," she moaned. "Maliss, I'm cummin', I'm cumin,'" she said, as she got even louder, reaching her final climax. She was so lost in the moment, she never even heard Ayesha creeping up behind her.

"Bitch! What the fuck is you doin', you dumb, stupid bitch!"

"Oh my God, girl. You scared the shit outta me," Santanna said, staring down the barrel. Ayesha smacked her across the face with the butt of her pistol.

"Bitch! Have you lost fuckin' mind?" Ayesha lowered the pistol down on Santanna's face again, causing her skin to bruise and bleed instantly. "Bitch, I thought my husband was in here fuckin' yo' triflin' ass, and you in here masturbatin' off his damn pictures!" She smacked her again, this time using her hand.

All Santanna knew to do was cover her face and head to block the repeated blows. "I'm, sorry . . . I—

But, Before she could get another word out, Ayesha delivered a hard blow that knocked her out cold.

"Stupid bitch gotta get the fuck up outta here right fuckin' now! This hoe got me fucked up! What the fuck she think! This shit ain't no fuckin' joke! 'Sposed to be my damn homie and shit." Ayesha went on and on, cussing and fussing, angrily. Then, she was startled by the vibrating sounds of Santanna's phone.

Since Santanna was unconscious on the floor with the dildo still in her hand, Ayesha picked up the phone when her curiosity got the best of her. "Oh, no the fuck this bitch didn't!" she said loudly.

"What happened, Mommy?" Gabbie said from the door.

"Nothin' baby. Go back to your room and I'll be there in a minute."

Ayesh grabbed a bottle of cold water from the mini-fridge that sat in the huge guest bathroom, and poured it in Santanna's face. "Wake yo' lame ass up, bitch, and get the fuck out my shit right now! I should kill your low-down, backstabbing ass," she said, allowing the tears to run freely down her face. "And then you had the nerves to tell Lil' Wee Wee where we lay our head at, 'cause yo' nasty ass been fuckin' him too?"

"I'm-I'm sorry, I know-I-I," Santanna stuttered to say.

"Bitch, I don't wanna hear no excuses. Get up, and get the fuck out!" Ayesha drew her foot back as far as she could and kicked her in the face with all the power she could muster up, bursting Santanna's top and bottom lips wide open. "Bitch, go get your daughter and get the fuck outta my house, *now!*"

The children peeped in from the doorway. They were both crying and hugging one another.

"Gabbie, didn't I tell you to go in the damn room and wait for me?"

The girls took off rurming as Santanna gathered her and her dauther's belongings. Next, she went to Gabbie's room and grabber her daughter by the hand. As she made her way toward the front door, Ayesha was close in tow. When she opened the door, Mailss was just pulling in the driveway and a black Impala was driving by.

"Damn, 'Tanna, what happened to you and where y'all goin'?" he asked curiously.

"She going where she qoing. Now get your ass in here," Ayesha said with a lot of attitude.

"Who the fuck you talkin' to?" Maliss said, looking her in the eyes. "Fuck wrong wit' you? Did you see that car pass when I pulled in?"

"No, I wasn't paying attention," she lied.

"Aight, well I'ma get on my phone and see what's up. I ain't never seen it around here before," he said.

"Mama, where we going?" Santanna's daughter cried as she was led out the house.

"Home, baby." She answered in a low voice as she pulled her by the hand,

"Why we walking? Did I do something wrong?" the little girl asked.

"No, baby." Santanna started to cry.

"Well, what's wrong, Mama?" her daughter questioned again, as she squeezed her mother's hand tightly.

"Nothing, I'm just happy you're getting so big, baby girl." As she walked to the curb, comforting her daughter, she decided to text Lil' Wee Wee:

Santanna: Where you at? I need you to come get me.

Lil' Wee Wee: on my way. He texted back.

CHAPTER 15

One week later…

"This is B. Armstrong, and I'm Allen Jones, and this is the 10:00 channel 10 news. First, we have video footage from last week's shooting: as you can see, the suspect's vehicle is a black Trans Am, and the suspect has been identified as a black male, around five feet nine, weighing about 180–210 pounds, with low hair. If anyone knows anything about this hidious crime, please call Crime Stoppers at 1-800-Crime-Stopper. There is a seven thousand five hundred three dollar reward out for any information that leads to a conviction. Again, that number is 1-800-Crime-Stopper."

Dirt Bag turned the television off. "Look at this shit. They got a check over a nigga's head and shit," he said.

"Man, fuck all that. They can't really tell who that is," Lil' Suwhoop said,

"Shit, that's easy for you to say yo' picture not the one up there, nigga."

"Nah, I'm just sayin' tho', don't panic, bruh. We good. The streets know how we rockin', and they know not to be rattin', feel me?"

"Shit, time will tell, homie, time will tell." Right in the middle of their conversing, there was a knock on the door

"Yeah, who that?" Lil' Suwhoop asked aggressively, instantly clutching his 9mm. He wondered who would come by without checking on first.

***

"Hi, this is Lisa Jones."

"And I'm Sherry Nunezz, and this is Channel 12 News at 11:00. Today's top story, in Asbury, Phenix City, Alabama, in

a middle-class neighborhood, a man was found hanging from a light pole with multiple stab wounds and, what appeared to be, chicken wire wrapped around his neck. A sign that read, 'no snitching allowed' was stapled to his chest. We have Melanie Rice live on the scene. Go ahead, Melanie."

"Yes, I'm reporting live in Asbury at one of the most horrific scenes I've ever witnessed in my 31 years of living. As you can see behind me, the fire marshalls have just cut the male down."

"Do they have an idea of who the person is, Melanie?" Lisa asked from the studio.

"Unm, no, they've identified him as being male, but I'll let Lieutenant Barns tell you more." Melanie stepped aside as a burly man in uniform came forth, in front of the camera.

"Yes, thank you. Well, the victim has been identified as a male figure and by fingerprint we have his name, yet we're not releasing that information as of yet. But along with the way the victim died, investigators have also discovered that the man's genitels had been cut off and stuffed inside his mouth. But again, once his family is contacted we will release a name."

"So, is there anything else you can tell us, Lieutentant?" Sherry inquired from the studio.

"At this time, all I can say is that this particular person was already a person of interest to our department, and that I'm sad it had to end like this for him. My heart goes out to his family."

"Any suspects or persons of interest in this case?" Melanie interjected.

"As of right now, we have no leads, but to the person responsible for this," Lt. Burns looked into the camera, *"we will find you, and you will be prosecuted to the fullest extent of the law. That is all I have right now, Ms. Rice."*

"Okay, and thank you for that information Lt. Burns, sir. There you have it. Reporting live, Melanie Rice. Back to you Lisa."

"Thank you, Melanie. Well, as you've heard, there are no reported suspects or witnesses. If you have any inforrnation on this matter, please feel free to contact Crime Stoppers at 1-800-Crime-Stopper. There is a $20,000 reward out for any information that leads to a conviction. We do not want anyone in our community with these horrific capabilities, " Lisa Jones said.

"Well coming up next, " Sherry chimed in, *"the employment rate percentages are going up, and after we come back, Bill will have an update on the five-day forecast."*

J-Rack turned the television off. "Damn, they fuck that boy around bad. I wonder how Lil' Rod taking it," he said to Red Dog.

"Fuck them niggas. Shit, that's better for us. Nigga shoulda hung both of them niggas on the pole, for real," Red Dog said. The two men bursted out laughing. "That's real. We gonna put a team together to get him out the way and take all he got. Fuck all that, bruh."

"Now you talkin' my talk," J-Racks said.

***

"Dang, did you see that?" Amy asked Lil' Rod in reference to the news report.

"Yeah, boo, that's fucked up," Lil' Rod replied. "They didn't have to do ol' boy like that."

"Yeah, but didn't that look like Lil' Fred, baby?"

"Why you say some shit like that?" he asked.

"Because of how he was dressed," Amy said.

Lil' Rod thought about it and reached for his phone to call Lil' Fred's number. When the voice message came on he hung up and tried calling twelve more times, getting the same result.

"Damn, he ain't answering either," he told Amy, "let me get up and go check on things," Lil' Rod said.

"Nigga you crazy ass hell. You ain't goin' nowhere else tonight. We locked in until the morning," Amy said, fighting with Rod to keep him in bed for the night.

"Fuck wrong wit' you, tryna leave me here all by myself with a crazy man on the loose." Amy tangled Rod in the sheets and cuddled closer to him. Rod kissed her on the forehead. "Your scary ass self."

"So. You saw that shit on the news. I'm glad I got a gangsta for a hubby, though," she said, easing her head underneath the covers to give him a head massage.

Lil' Rod reclined more as his erection grew in her warm mouth. "Yeah, bae, just like that," he moaned in satisfaction. He smiled to himself, happy to hear there were no suspects regarding the murder. Amy gave him super slow neck and it was just what Lil' Rod needed to ease his mind. He lit a blunt and enjoyed the ride.

CHAPTER 16

COLEMAN USP 1

"Shit, to whoever say he don't, I got thirty books on Scottie that he 4-5-6 in the next four rolls," Paper Boi Rari said.

"I want money, lots and lots of money, so don't be askin' me why I wanna be rich!" Scottie sang his favorite song by Calloway as he rolled the dice.

"Pick up, Paper Boi," Scottie said, confidently.

"Nigga, I ain't got no bet yet," Paper Boi replied. "Man, hold the dice!"

"Hell nah, you ain't on the dice, bruh," Scrap, who was fading Scottie on the roll, spoke up.

"Y'all broke ass niggas bet thirty, then," Paper Boi Rari announced.

"I hear you, Paper Boi. Talk that shit, nigga," City Boi Freak said. "You got yo' bread up, huh?"

"Hell yeah, bruh. They call me Paper Poi Rari. I run it up fast, RPMs in the red, nigga."

City Boi laughed at the humor, and with all the excitment and commotion going on, Scottie was able to switch the dice to the pair of loaded ones he kept on him. He was better than Houdini with the quick switch of the hands.

Scottie was from Boynton Beach, Florida, off Cherry Hill. He was an old school player that knew the game better than anyone. An expert at the con and talking shit game, he was 45 years old with dark skin. Everybody loved *and* hated Scottie, equally. He stayed drunk, and was always calling niggas out, and he cussed more than a sailor.

"I bet he don't 4-5-6 in the next two," J-Red said.

"Bet that!" Paper Boi said, throwing his thirty books down, J-Red threw his down too.

"Let me hit that bottle, Paper," Scottie said, reaching for the water bottle containing the home-made liquor.

"Here you go, bruh." Paper passed him a 20 ounce water bottle filled with moonshine Paper Boi had made. The moonshine had been noted as the best on the compound—well, next to the best, because he couldn't out-shine his teacher, Blu.

Blu was the master of prison alcohol. He was from the outskirts of Atlanta, Georgia, and proud of his talent.

"Ooh-wee," Scottie said after taking a large swig. "Damn! Now that's that gas right there, nigga. Boy, you got the best on the pound, Paper. I don't care what nobody say."

"Man, roll the dice," Scrap yelled.

"Man, I'm 'bout to roll the dice, just hold on. Hey, Paper, you got anymore of that juice?" Scottie asked.

"Yeah, I got four more twentys, bruh," Paper replied.

"Let me get one right now," he told Paper. A 20-ounce water bottle of shine went for twenty books on the compound, which was the equivelent to $70 dollars,

"Aight, I'ma match one wit' you . . . nah, fuck it. I feel good so I'ma go 'head and match two wit' you, bruh," Paper Boi said, "but you better hit your point, old nigga," he added.

"I got you. Let me go on and roll." Scottie stepped up and did his famous dance, while singing his favorite song. As he released the dice, he said, "Pick up your money, Paper," and the dice rolled and stopped 4-5-6.

"Aww!" The crowd went crazy.

"Nigga, I told you!" Paper Boi said excitedly.

"Man, they can't fuck wit' you, Boi." Scottie picked up his money as Scrap walked off fussing.

"Man, let me hit that bottle. Shit, that was my re-up money damn," J-Red said. Everybody erupted in laughter as Paper passed him the bottle. He turned it up and down. "Whooo, man, yeah, bruh, you got that heat," he said to Paper.

"Let me hold five books until we get in the unit, bruh," City Boi said.

"Man, I ain't got it right now," Paper answered

"What? Nigga, you just won thirty. What the hell you talkin' 'bout. Man, you need to stop holdin' so damn tight. I got you when we get back inside. I just need to handle something right fast before we leave."

"Shit, you knew that before you came out," Paper responded.

"Don't worry 'bout it, bruh, I got something for your ass, you stingy ass nappy head ass nigga," City said with anger.

Paper Boi was a slim, light-skinned, little dude with long ass dreads in his head called wicks. Wicks didn't actually twist like regular dreads because all you had to do was grow them and let them lock.

"Here go five books, nigga, and I want my shit soon as we get in or you gettin' ran up top," Paper Boi Rari said with a serious look. Both men knew he was only joking with his friend, City Boi.

"Nigga, I ain't worried 'bout' it. My paperwork good. I can go anywhere," City stated.

"Man, don't none of y'all say shit else to me, bitch-ass niggas. All y'all, fuck boys!" Scottied shouted in a drunken rage.

"Aww, shit, there go Scottie. He all crunk up again," City said to Paper. It's yo' fault 'cause you the one who gave him that liquid gas, now look at him."

"Man, sit yo' ass down somewhere, Scottie," Paper Boi said.

"Man, fuck you! Kiss my ass, nigga," Scottie shouted.

Paper Boi laughed. He never paid Scottie any attention when he got drunk. "Alright now, I'ma make one of these lil' niggas get on you a out here, old man," Paper said.

"Man, fuck you! These sorry ass niggas ain't 'bout to do shit to me!"

Paper laughed again. Then the announcment for the ten-minute activity move came over the loud speaker. "Grab them bottles from off the bench," Paper Boi said to City. "I'm gone. I gotta get on this horn for a minute and see what's goin' on out there. You know I ain't been heard in a while," he said.

"Yeah, me too. I'm 'bout to hit 1st Degree up, see what's out there," City added.

"You have a collect call from. . ." *'Beep'* . . . Lil' Rod pressed 5.

"What up wit' it, cuz?" Paper Boi Rari said.

"Shit, a whole lot, nigga. It's smokin' out here," Lil' Rod informed him, referring to being under investigation by the police.

"Oh, yeah?"

"Yeah, man. Lil' Fred got murked. This shit wild out here right now," Lil' Rod said, then went on to tell Paper about everything else that was going on in the hood.

"You have a collect call from . . ." *Beep.* . . 1st Degree accepted the call right away.

"What it do, lil' one?" City Boi said.

"Shit, just makin' ends meet out here. A nigga got robbed in the Gump and shit after a show at Club Gwaped Up."

"What, nigga," City Boi Freak exclaimed. "See, that's why I don't fuck wit' them niggas up there, bruh. They too thirsty, my nigga."

"Man, I think Swolehead set it up, my nigga," 1st Degree said.

"Nah, that ain't him, bruh. He gettin' paper and he respect the hustle. I know him, bruh," City Boi said.

Well if it wasn't him, somebody caught a nigga slippin'. Got the shit all on the internet and shit. But fuck all that, I sent the cards off Thursday," 1st Degree said.

"Oh, aight then, bet that up. I should get them Monday or Tuesday then."

"They don't pass out mail on the weekend. But, aight, bruh, I ain't gonna hold you up, my nigga," City said. Before he could speak his last peace, the institution's alarm rang loudly over the dorm speakers.

"Everybody on the ground now!" an officer yelled.

"Man, damn! Everytime I hear from you this shit happen, don't it," 1st Degree said.

"Hell yeah, and this time we might be down for a minute too," City said, watching an inmate butcher another with a homemade knife the size of a lawnmower blade.

"What the fuck is that?" Lil' Rod said, hearing the blaring alarm over the phone.

"Man, that's the duces. That mean we 'bout to get locked down. Some shit done happened and, by the sound of it, a cop was involved," Paper Boi said.

"Get on the ground now!" the loud speaker commanded.

"Damn, I thought a police car pulled up or something," Lil' Rod said, referring to the loud whirling noises he heard in the background of the prison.

"Well, it was good hearin' from you, cuz. Stay safe, nigga, and stay prayed up," Paper spoke.

"Alright, bet. You stay safe too, nigga. And come on home, we waitin' for you, cuz."

"Bet that. One love." Paper Boi hung up.

"Get to your cells!" the CO in the unit yelled.

"Man, all types of shit happenin' out there," Paper Boi said to City on their way to their cells.

"Yeah, on my end, too. But it's show time. You ready to perform?" City Boi Freak asked Paper as the CO locked their cell door.

"Hell yeah!" Paper responded.

One hour later. . .

"Whoa, now," City Boi called to an officer as he made his hourly rounds around the tier. "What happened out there?"

"Four inmates on three COs," the officer said.

"What?" City and Paper responded from inside their cell.

"Man, I knew it was big, but damn!" City said.

"Hell yeah," Paper added.

"But fuck it, we should be straight this week," City told Paper. "Check it, I got three cards on the way. That's thirteen bands a card. I want nine a card and you keep four, bruh. That way I can pay bruh for doin' it for me and keep him motivated to keep workin', feel me?" City said.

"Yeah, I got you," Paper said, as he did the math in his head. He knew he could make at least twenty a card with his hustle game and stretch some money out of it, and have way more then what City Boi was talking about.

"Don't fuck this up, bruh," City said. "Cuz I gotta pay for this shit, feel me?"

"Man, I got it," Paper replied.

"You said that shit the last six times, nigga. I'm for real right here tho', or I'ma have to cut yo' water off ," City said.

"Alright, bruh, damn. I got you," Paper said repeated.

CHAPTER 17

The manager at Strokers was a tall red-bone with hazel eyes, short blond hair, C-cup breasts, and little waist with a big ol' onion booty, enough booty to make the whole city cry.

"So when did you notice this foul smell?" Agent Malone asked the manager.

"Well, maybe yesterday or perhaps, it was the day before," she said.

"Okay, I see," agent Malone replied.

"What about this truck?" Agent Patricia asked. "I know you noticed it here day after day, right?"

"Well, yeah, I saw the truck. You couldn't help but see it. But this is a well known establishment, ma'am. By the time we get here to unlock the doors, the parking lot is already filled with employees, customers, or window shoppers, if you get my drift. Nothing seemed, or looked, outta place until the foul smell became noticable. Even when we close we never think to check 'cause in this business everything goes," the manager said.

"I see," Agent Patricia finally said, listening attentively.

"Well, we have a positive ID of this guy. His name is Donte A. Williams. It's strange 'cause we been trying to contact him ourselves," Malone said. "But, for now, let me have your name and personal phone number just in case we have further questions. And here's my card. If you think of anything else, please don't hesitate to contact us. Thank you."

"Will do, and thank you. My number is 404-697-8151. I go by Mesha Millz. Y'all come back and don't y'all be strangers now. We have somebody here for everybody," she said. Like the true businesswoman she was, she always promoting the business.

"Maybe we will," Agent Malone said, poking his chest out.

"And maybe we won't," Agent Patricia said, pulling Malone by the arm to leave as the Crime Scene Investigation unit went in to finish cleaning up the crime scene.

ATL Federal Building . . .

"You think we'll come up with a lead? Agent Patricia asked.

"Maybe so . . . I sure hope so 'cause something is tellin' me that this triple homicide and this Stroker homicide is connected," Malone said. "We've got cases up the ass that are still unsolved. We still got the southside shit too, and something has to give. All this heroin and fentanyl shit has got the city going crazy, and it's all that fuckin' Maleek's fault, I'm sure of it. Thing is, our supervisor won't let us get him. But look, it's two-thirty in the morning, and I'm still at work."

"Yeah, he won't let us get him 'cause we don't have anything solid on him. Anyways, fuck him till we get something on him that'll stick. So, I don't want to hear shit else about him," Patricia said.

"Yeah, alright, but I'll get that bastered if it's the last thing I do, you can believe that," Malone said with finality.

A knock on the door startled them both.

"Yeah, come on in," Malone said.

"What's up wit' it, Malone? How you're doing, Patricia?" Agent Smith asked walking in.

"Very well indeed," Patricia said. She licked her lips and blushed.

"Man, I feel a little better now that you've walked in," Malone said. "So I hope you have good news for me since we have no direct contact with you. I stay worried to death with all this madness in the city, you know."

"Ya, I'm Gucci, sir. I been in the field for a while now so it's become my life, and since I value my life, I protect it with great care, feel me?" Smith said.

Agent Smith was dark-skinned with a Caesar cut, deep waves and snow-white teeth, a real hoe catcher. He had major sauce, could adapt to any hood, and he'd pass for a real street nigga—that was because it was where he'd earned his beginning, yet soon chose the big brother role after getting jammed in a big car stealing operation.

He turned government informant by giving up valuable information which assisted in the dismissal of his case. Soon after, he was hired as a field agent for the FBI due to his adaptability and place in deep cover.

Agent Smith fit the streets perfectly. He was aggressive, had charisma, proper swagger, and could slick talk on any topic. Weighing just under 200lbs and standing at a solid six feet, he was already imposing on his own, the badge just gave him room to move.

"So, what you got for me, Agent Smith?" Malone asked. Agent Smith went on to debrief his co-worker on the valuable information he'd obtained so far.

**

"Hold up, Spook, I'd let you see 'em, but the shit already gone. Matter-of-fact, that's what I'm waiting on right now. I'm 'bout to slide in a minute," Dirt bag said as he texted on his phone.

"You was 'bout to what?" Lil' Suwhoop asked.

"Man, fall back. I'm 'bout to go pick this check up for the 70 real fast, you heard, blood." Dirt Bad grabbed the duffel bag and unzipped it for Spook to see what else he had inside it. Spook examined it real good but knew it was flex immediately. He was originally from New York, and certified when it came to designer clothes and jewelry. He stayed up on everything.

"Man, this some real good flex, nigga. Somebody gonna be real disappointed when they find out." Spook laughed.

"Yeah, that's why it ain't for you, nigga," Dirt Bag said, zipping the bag back up. He texted into his phone again, telling the anxious buyer to meet him at the Cheveron on South Blvd. They exchanged info as Spook went to the TV to put on his new single, Flavor Room the Kitchen.

"Shit, I'll be back. I'm finna get to the Chevron so I can see my vic pull up, feel me? Might have something for y'all when I get back," he said, heading to the door.

Dirt Bag was so tuned into his phone he hadn't noticed the line of men standing outside the window. In a matter of minutes they had burst the door down causing a loud explosion.

"Everybody down! Everybody down," the two masked men shouted as they entered the home. They were both armed with mini-assualt rifles.

Spook got put down instantly, face first. The heaviest masked man rushed Dirt Bag, kicking him in the face with his combat boot.

"Nigga, face the fuckin' floor!" he demanded.

Dirt Bag rolled over slowly. The man put his knee in Dirt Bag's back and hog tied him with percision while another man held them at gunpoint. One by one, Suwhoop and Spook were also tied.

"Who else in this bitch!" the tallest man said, as he entered in. No one said a word. "Check the place top and bottom," he told the big masked man, "that means everything!"

"Nigga, you know who we are?" Dirt Bag spoke. "You betta believe I'ma n—

The tall one kicked Dirt Bag in the mouth, then stomped his head to the floor with the hard soles of his Timberlands. A loud crack exploded from Dirt Bag. He hit the floor and laughed as if he hadn't felt a thing.

"Yeah, that's it, bitch boy! Now I'ma kill yo' hoe ass mama for not swallowin' yo' fuck ass!"

"All clear," another intruder shouted, coming from a room in the corner of the house.

"You sure?" the big man asked. He nodded and both men pulled their masks off. Lil' Suwhoo almost pissed his pants. Spook thought he'd seen a ghost. Dirt Bag knew he was dead without question.

Spook fell on his face so fast it looked as though he'd suddenly fainted. Dirt Bag rose to his knees and held his composure with a grimace. Death would be the only way he'd lie down.

"You see this nigga here, Hawk?" Maliss said, pointing at Dirt Bag.

"He a real thorough bred. Yep," Maliss shook his head in deep thought, wondering the best way to make him suffer. "Too bad he went against me instead of being with me. Such a waste of potental, partna. You dumb-smart, feel me? You use your energy the wrong way. Now it done caught up wit' you, lil' homie. I coulda made you millions, bruh. I fucks wit' the streets. I *am* the streets, partna. Why would you wanna bring harm to me? Then you tried to hurt my family? Oh, now that's personal." Maliss pulled the ratchet back on his Desert Eagle.

"Rule number one: Never try a real street nigga such as myself by fuckin' wit' his bitch, because a real street nigga, such as myself, will see that shit comin'." Maliss tapped Dirt

Bag against his head with the weapon as he spoke. "See, that's why you couldn't get to her. The truck was bulletproof and *she* didn't even know that. The best part was the cameras on the truck. Damn, what would I have done if it wasn't for that? Do anyone of y'all know?" No one said a word.

"Okay, since y'all all choked the fuck up at the moment, let me tell y'all real fast before I finish up here. First, I would've put out a bounty. Now, that woulda been risky you see, 'cause y'all woulda cost me time and money, and most importantly, an opportunity for a bitch-ass nigga to rat on me.

Thank God for technology, right, fellas?" Maliss chuckled, deviously, cool-like. "And you," he said with his focused now solely on Dirt Bag, "yo' dumb-smart ass all over Instagram like a show hoe tryna pop flyy. The site a dead giveaway for sweet niggas like you."

Maliss whipped the pistol across Dirt Bag's face. "Wet this bitch down!" he told Hawk .

Hawk went to the kitchen and turned the oven and stove on. Underneath the sink he found two cans of Raid roach spray and sat them on the kitchen counter. Next, he went into the nearby bathroom and came out with a bottle of rubbing alcohol. He dashed some on the couch and curtains, and poured the rest over Dirt Bag's head. "I'm 'bout to send yo' bitch-ass straight to hell, nigga, " Hawk said.

"Fuck you, pussy ass nigga," Dirt Bag said in defiance. Hawk stepped back and kicked him in the ribs, causing Dirt Bag to holler for revenge.

"Let me turn the wave on real fast," Hawk said. He ran in the kitchen and Lil' Suwhoop turned his head toward the couch and let the tears fall down his face, as he knew his life was at its end at the young age of 17. Spook said a silent prayer, asking God to look over his mother and father and four kids, plus his unborn that was on the way which he would never get to see.

Dirt Bag's menacing eyes stayed on Maliss the entire time. Maliss smiled at the man's fortitude. "Okay, bruh, that's a go in there. Let's blow this joint," Maliss said, laughing at his own crude joke. "Well, fellas, only the strong survive, my niggas, and the well-seasoned vets make it through this shit. You have to be a thinker, and you can't ever sleep. The only thing that comes to a sleeper is a dream . . . or a nightmare!" He struck a match and threw it on Dirt Bag. "Tell Satan I said better luck next time, you shoulda stayed in your lane, nigga."

Dirt Bag's entire body went ablaze. He hollered and screamed sounds that were unhuman in nature. All around, the entire house began to catch fire quickly. Maliss and Hawk placed on their masks and eased out of the house, leaving the three bound men to face an infernio.

Inside, Suwhoop and Spook had squirmed out of their ties, but by then the flames had reached the windows and had already started climbing the walls.

"C'mon, bruh, let's get outta here," Maliss said to Hawk who spun out of the area with haste. As they reached the bridge by Gateway Park, the loud explosion rattled the car windows. Maliss looked in the rearview, laughing. "Bruh, that's your signature right there," he said as Hawk turned on 85 north, en route to the Atlanta.

CHAPTER 18

Shit, I need 150 BM, homes. ASAP! Chad read the text. Then responded. *Bet that. Come to the Ritz Carlton.* He sent back. *What Room?* the text replied. *Just let me know when you here. I'll come to you, homes.* Chad send back. Chad had Shell help him trap when she wasn't at work or catering to his every need.

"You good, bae?" Shell asked him.

"Yeah, boo, I just need you to run this pack down when bruh pull up. Matter-of-fact, it'll be better if you was already down there, that way we'll have a visual on the area before he get here, just in case he decide to pull some funny shit, feel me?"

"Yeah, bae, sounds right to me. Do you need anything before I go down?" she asked, massaging his dick through his Saint Laurent trousers. She licked her lips with inclined interest.

"See, why you tryna start something when we got business to take care of," he said, squirming with excitement. "But, nah, I'm good for now. Fuck wit' me when you get back and we count this money. You know that makes my dick super hard."

"Alright, bae." Shell pecked him on the lips and headed out the door. Chad turned the plasma Smart TV on to HLN and popped a 30mg of Oxycontin, washing it down with some dirty Sprite.

"Hi, this is Robin Medows, and this is News Live for June 18, 2018, Monday. Today, we have a couple of headlines making national news. The first one is the House of Pain. The American Opioid epidemic. You've heard of Oxycotin, the pain medication, but did you know the company that makes and reaps the billions of dollars in profits it generates is owned by one secretive family. The Purdue family."

Chad's phone vibrated as an incoming text came in.

Shell: What kinda car he in bae.

Chad: A silver Benz. Red inside. Chad wrote back.

Shell: Oh. i see it now. Shell replied

Chad: Aight. what it look like boo?

Shell: He pulled up by himself so it seem safe but i got my piece with me. I'm good. She smiley-faced her message before sending it to Chad.

Chad: Aight, boo, be safe. That should be $4500. Nothin less.

Chad: Aight partna, I see you. Stay right there my bitch comin to ur whip. Make sure it's $4500 str8 up playa. He sent the message and rewound the DVR to the part of the newscast he'd missed, noticing his motions had slowed down due to the pills he'd taken.

"According to Forbes, a $14 Billion dollar fortune came from Oxycotin, the addictive, narcotic pain killer regarded by many public health experts as one of the most dangerous products ever sold on a mass scale. Since 1996, when drugs were bought to market by Purdue Pharma, the American brunch of the Sacklers' pharmaceutical empire, more than two hundred thousand people in the United States have died from overdoses of Oxycotin and other prescription painkillers."

Shell texted and let Chad know everything was good on her end, and that she and Maliss were on their way up.

Chad read the text and continued to listen to Robin give her news report. In his mind he saw the dollar signs in the perscription drug trade as a way out.

"...thousands more have died after starting on a perscription opioid and then switching to a drug with cheaper street prices, such as heroin," the news anchor woman continued.

The hotel door opened and Shell escorted Maliss in. "Okay, bae, we good. I'ma put this up. Maliss, make yourself at home," Shell said, heading to the master bedroom.

"What's up wit' it, my boy? Maliss said, giving Chad dap.

"Shit, you got it, big bruh. But hold on a minute, I'm on this news real fast, talkin' 'bout the opioid epidemic."

"Oh, yeah?" Maliss said, sitting down in the Lay-Z-Boy. Shell came back in and sat on his lap as he tuned his attention on the rest of the story.

"According to the Centers for Disease Control," Robin Medes said, *"fifty-three thousand Americans died from opioid over-doses in 2017 alone, more than the thirty-six thousand who died in car crashes in 2016, or the thirty-five thousand who died from gun violence that same year. This past July, Donald Trump's commission on combating drug addiction and the opioid crisis, led by New Jersey's governor Chris Christie . . .*

"Man, fuck Donald Trump!" Maliss stated out of nowhere. Chad and Shell looked at him and smiled.

". . . declared that opiods were killing roughly 142 Americans each day, a tally vividly described as a 9/11, every three weeks."

"Dayumm," they all said nearly in unison.

Robin continued: *"The epidemic has also exacted a crushing financial toll according to a study published by the American Public Health Association, using thata from 2013– before the epidemic entered its current, more virulent phase. The total economic burden from opioid use stood at about $80 billion, adding together health cost, criminal justice cost, and GOP losses from drug-dependent Americans leaving the workforce."*

Maliss listened closely, nodding his head, already devising a plan on the street take-over, and a pharmis lick at the same time.

"Tobacco remains, by a significant multiple, the country's most lethal product, responsible for some 48,000 deaths per year. But although billions have been made from tobacco, cars, and firearms, it's not clear that any of those enterprises have generated a family fortune from a single product that even closely approaches the Sackler's haul from Oxycotin.

The Fords, Hewletts, Packards, Johnson, Walmart, all those families put their names on their products because they were proud, according to Keith Humphreys, a professor of psychiatry at Stanford University School of Medicine, who has written extensively about the opioid crisis," Robin said.

"The Slackers have hidden their connection to their product. They don't call it 'Slacker Pharma.' They don't call their pills 'Sackler pills.' And when they're questioned, they say, 'Well, it's a privately held firm, we're family and we like to keep our privacy, you understand.' No we don't," Robin Medows said. "There you have it, America, the House of Pain, killing so many of our families across the U.S., with the producers who don't want to take the blame. The Sacklers. Brothers who came from a family of Jewish immigrants in Flatbush, Brooklyn. Authur, Mortimer, and Raymond Sackler, the billionaire founders. More on this topic tonight at 11 :00," she ended.

"Damn, that's that bread right there now, 'cause they have to have it no matter what," Chad said. "Shit, we need to hit this full fledged, huh, big bruh?" he asked Maliss who already had his hands on some, stacked up and ready to go.

"Hell yeah. So what's up, lil' homie, you ready to open shop on this new money?"Maliss enticed.

"C'mon now, bruh, you already know what's up wit' me. We already been playin' in the pussy, now I'm ready to fuck somethin'!"

"Well, let me look into it and I'ma get back at you," Maliss said as Robin Medows came back on with her second headline story.

"Our second story comes out of Montgomery, Alabama," Robin spoke, catching Maliss' attention.

"An explosion off of South Blvd, as of right now, has been labeled a terriorist threat . . . " Maliss' eyes shot open wide with shock. *". . . these explosions seem to be taking place in multiple cities within a 200 mile radius. The local FBI in the region are looking into this incident very closely, as well as local department agencies in the area. Three bodies have been discovered burned beyond*

recognition with limbs detached and missing. As of now, no one has been identified among the victims.

Forensics and medical examiners sent DNA samples to the lab for further review. There are no witness nor suspects responsible as of this reporting.

Anyone with any information are asked to call into their local police department, Robin bowed and shook her head with grief. Oh, Lord, please bless our counrty Up next, we have the weather forcast for the week from meteroligist Kevin Mole. . . ."

"Damn, that shit getting' real out there," Chad said.

"Yeah, that's why I always tell you, safety first. No sleep, nigga. Stay alert," Maliss said.

Chad nodded. "That's big facts."

"I know you already know, that's why you gonna have to lay off that dirty mud, bruh, for real. This shit is for keeps out here, homes." Maliss laid into Chad.

By the time he'd stood up to leave, he had all types of thoughts swimming around in his head. He was ready to find the Sacklers by any means necessary and get that receipt, he also had the big rig heist lined up to get some cigarettes, and then he had Johnny the jewelry man and store owner to see about. To say Maliss was after a major check would've been an understatement. He was like that boy Kevin Gates who said, "'I got six jobs, I don't get tired.'"

"Show yo' right, big bruh. As soon as I heal all the way up I'ma quit, that's my word. I need my life so I can get these checks to carry these generations on, so I'm tryna keep going." He looked at Shell and she smiled.

"That's real, homes. I'ma get back at you, but I'm glad to see you comin' along, nigga. Come lock this door, Shell," Maliss said, as he walked toward the door made his exit.

By the time Shell returned, Chad had fallen into a deep nod.

CHAPTER 19

Hawk was waiting at the spot for Maliss to pull up when Maliss pulled in suddenly. Screeching tires against the gravel, he hit the breaks hard. The spot had been broken into and they had taken a hard hit. Although they had insurance on the building, all the drugs were gone, and someone had just hit them for a gold mine.

"What the fuck!" Maliss shouted, as he jumped out of his vehicle. He paced back and forth, taking long strides, visibly fuming. "Whoever did this is gonna die, bruh, believe that.

They whole family gon' get it!" Hawk said.

The back door had been wielded through and the front glass windows and doors had been busted out. Everything inside had been completely cleaned out.

"Oh, whoever did this was a pro, huh." Maliss said. "Nigga deactivated a nigga shit, huh? Aight, smart ass niggas, let's see how smart you really are." Maliss went inside the building to the control panel and rewound the cameras. Hawk followed closely behind.

Instantly, they saw six people pull into the lot in a Ford Super Duty with an attached RV trailer hooked to it. All the men jumped out wearing hoodies, concealing their faces. They stormed the building as a unit, then the camera went black.

"Oh yeah, y'all pretty smart," Maliss said bitterly, as Hawk watched closely trying to pick up on every little detail. "But y'all still ain't smart as me," Maliss added with a sneer.

Fifteen seconds later, the cameras switched back on due to the back-up batteries he'd installed. "There you stupid muthafuckas go," he said, watching as two of the men posted as lookouts. Two others held, what appeared to be, a blanket over another one as he torched the door. Minutes later they were in, rushing straight to the electronics and speakers in the house. Then for some reason one of the men lifted his mask.

"Bingo!" Maliss said. He stopped the tape and rewound it to zoom in on the man's face. Maliss was deep in the streets, top lip deep, so he knew damn near everybody in the underworld, making this violation an automatic suicide for everyone involved.

"Okay, these lil' fuckers gotta have balls to try niggas like us, bruh! Like we ain't 'bout that life," Hawk said, as he leaned in trying to see if recognized any of the men. "That's Flat Head Boyz, huh?"

Maliss nodded silently, already thinking about Roe Black and how to use him.

"They gotta know they all dead, right," Hawk added. However, it wasn't a question but a confirmation that all involved would pay.

"Man, you already know what the lick is, bruh. They done fucked up, point-blank-period. Nigga, that's blood money they takin' and don't even know it. What the fuck wrong wit' these new niggas?" Maliss questioned.

Then laughed as he dialed the police from his phone with the intention of phoning the insurance company next.

***

"Hell yeah, Twan. We just killed them wit' this one! Yeah, yeah, that way," Mizzie said, dabbing on his crew in excitement.

Twan was the leader, and due to a snitch in the circle they had all just gotten out of the Feds for fucking with the car industry. They were in desperate need of some fast cash and decided *The Spot* was as good as any. They would sell the speakers and make a killing really fast, along with putting some extra amps and sounds in their own cars.

Twan was also the oldest and he was just a young 22-year-old himself. He had just finished installing the touch screens in his ZL1 Camaro on 26s. Light-skinned, six feet two with a fully tatted body, he kept his hair in a mohawk dread like a Shota.

Mizzie was only 19. He was short and stood five-two. His sleeves and face were tatted and he had shoulder length dreads.

Rocky was dark-skinned with beginner dreads and tattoos, and he was six feet one inch tall.

Itchy was 21, and he was the only foreigner in the hood because he was Chinese. He had full-body tattoos with piercings, and stood taller than everyone at six feet five. His hair was matted with eighteen wicks.

Rondo was a 20-year-old with midnight black skin and long dreads, and he tats everywhere. Lil' Mac was the shortest of them all standing a little over four feet. He was mixed with Black and Native American. He was 19 with tats and the only one who of them who didn't have dreads. Instead, he rocked a low-boy hair cut with ocean waves, and kept a Mac 10 on him at all times—that was how he'd gotten his name.

Their entire crew had gotten a flathead screwdriver tatted on them to rep their mob. Everyone in the city knew them for having some of the flyyest cars. They were better than the predators who played in movie *Gone in 60 Seconds* . . . for them, it was more like, gone in six seconds!

"Boy, look at these 15s, nigga," Twan said, as he proceeded to use his power drill to undo the speakers. He had placed his gun in the secret compartment behind it to avoid it being found in the event of a police search. "I'm 'bout to beat the city down with these bad boys!" He unlatched one of the speakers and stashed his gun behind it.

"Nigga, I put four 12s in the Vette," Rondo said, "with the thousand watt Fosgate amp, boy. So you already know what that do," he added.

"What the fuck," Twan stated, as he pulled his hand back from the speaker. His hand had touched something inside the box. Tilting the box, he looked inside it.

"What the fuck is this?" he asked as he pulled a duct taped rectangular-type square out of it. He frowned and looked at his crew. He looked back in the speaker and saw five more packages. A wide smile spread across his face because whatever it was, he was the lucky one who had gotten it, and it was all his.

He pulled the rest of the packages out and poked one of them with the screwdriver. A brown powder substance began falling through the hole. The mere thought of what it could be caused his dick to get hard.

"Heroin . . .a whole brick . . . oh shit, oh shit! I'm rich bitch," he yelled. "I'm fuckin' rich! This a whole thang right here, and there's five more inside. Y'all niggas must can't see or somethin'. Plus, I picked these speakers myself." Twan laughed so hard he fell on the floor. He poked another one and this time a pink, chalky substance spilled out. He scratched his head . . . "I know this ain't that pink Molly . . . it can't be ..."

He dapped a little on his pinky and tasted it. From the smile on his face, one would've thought he was a kid on Christmas day. "Yes, sir-ree it is!" By now, he was breathing so hard he almost hyperventilated. "Oh my God it's on now, my niggas. Y'all don't fuckin' understand, it's fuckin' on!" I'm 'bout to blow this citythe fuck up!"

"You do know we all in on this lick, right?" Mizzie asked.

"Yeah, what's up wit' it?" Twan said, already feeling the grudge.

"I'm just sayin' . . . you already know how we rock, so don't start the larceny, bruh. "Man, fuck all that, nigga. It's six of us and six of them. All of us 'bout to get one so you need to pick which one you want while you over there jumpin' for joy and shit," Mizzie said.

Twan poked the third package and some fine tiny crystals fell out. "Man, hold up, hold the fuck up ..." He tasted it. "Yep, straight ice in this bitch! Yeah, bitch, that way!" He dabbed them all and realized he'd hit the mega jackpot. He closed the trunk of his car, leaving everything inside.

"Now, what was that, homes?" He looked at all of them with a look they had never seen before; however, Itchy was already in his vehicle using the drill to open his speakers. He found eight bricks inside.

"Hey, man, I'm loaded too," he yelled out.

Everyone stopped arguing and ran to their perspective cars, and realized there was dope stasted everywhere.

"Aww, man! We strapped now, boy. That lick shit over wit'," Twan said, still smiling from ear-to-ear. He thought about all the systems and speakers they had sold throughout the hood and realized they would now have to go around and steal them all back. The crew began opening all the packages they had found.

"Hey, man, we got spice in this bitch too! Nigga, whoever shit this is gonna be mad as hell. This shit gotta be worth millions and we gonna have to lay low for a while too, bruh," Lil' Mac said.

Click-Clack.

The unforgiving sound of the ratchet echoed loudly in Lil' Mac's ear as the pistol pressed firmly against his head.

"Yeah, y'all bitches 'bout lay real low, my nigga," Maliss told him.

"Don't nobody move!" Hawk said through clenched teeth. He walked around with a sawed-off shotgun, and pointed it in each of their faces.

"Know what I'm talkin' 'bout. I'm talkin' six feet low, shawty!" Maliss said. "Everybody down, now! Bitch ass, stupid niggas! How y'all gon' break in my shit and think I'm not gon' find out? Stop playin', boys."

He walked over while holding Lil' Mac at gun point and pushed him over with the rest of the crew. Ordering them to sit in a circle, he smacked him across the back of the head. "Never take your mask off in a lick, bruh," he told Lil' Mac, as he fell to his knees from the blow.

"It's gon' cost you your life unless you take everybody life who saw you, ya heard?" Lil' Mac nodded, rubbing the back of his head.

"Get yo' lil' bitch ass up, 'cause you got work to do, nigga. And all my shit better be here, too. Get to opening all the speakers and grab that car cover right there," Maliss ordered Lil' Mac, "and load everything right there, and hurry the fuck up! Make sure you get my shit out of them cheap ass cars too, nigga." Maliss then looked over the rest of the Flat Head Boyz who were on their knees with Hawk standing over them. "Y'all can thank him for y'all down fall."

"Man, fuck all that rap shit and get the fuck on!" Twan yelled. Maliss raised his weapon quickly and shot Twan in the face with the silenced Draco, blowing the back of his head clean off.

"Holy shit," Mizzie screamed.

"Shut the fuck up, pussy!" Maliss aimed and sent three rounds into his head, silencing him immediately. "Anybody got anything else to say? 'Cause I'm really not tryna hear it," he said.

Everyone was silent with their hands behind their heads. Lil' Mac went to work without hesitation after witnessing the death of two of his best friends. It had taken him a little over two hours to finish de-attaching all the stereo equipment.

Once he'd placed the last package of dope down, Maliss told him to go kneel over by his partners with his hands behind his head. He did so and almost gagged at the smell and sight of his homies brain matter and bits of skull spread over the concrete, knowing his fate was similar.

With Maliss on guard, Hawk tied all the equipment to the truck, with the Lil' Mac assisting him. Lil' Mac saw this as an opportunity since he was still strapped with his weapon.

However, just as soon as he walked past Maliss, with the speed of lightening, he spun around and blew Lil' Mac's head off with such quick speed pieces of his head hit the ground before his body did. Maliss then sprayed bullets into the rest of the helpless crew. Seeing nothing but blood flowing from their motionless bodies, he knew it was time to join Hawk in the truck. The two drove off without so much as a second glance.

Paper Boi Rari

CHAPTER 20

You know we 'bout that stick / that stick talk / you know we 'bout that lick talk / that lick talk. . . . Lil' Wee-Wee rapped along with Future as he clutched his Draco with the fifty round drum attached to it, in his lap. He was six cars behind his victim's triple black Jeep SRT-8.

"Today is it, I knew it . Do your homework and you'll pass every time," he said to himself. Thanks to Santanna, he'd been following his target for the past few weeks. "Thank you bitch!" he shouted. "Now it looks like it's finally gonna pay off. This shit gotta be done right, 'cause it's two of them. But fuck that, I got fifty niggas wit' me, and it's all about the element of surprise.

Plus, I'm not from 'round here, so don't nobody know me. Shit, I can get down how I want to, *and* I'm by myself. That's four pluses on my end. . . . Yeah, I'm good," he said, preparing and amping himself up for the work ahead.

"I'm tellin' you, Hawk, this gonna be the key to a billion dollar generation for us, bruh," Maliss said.

"My nigga, you know I'm always down wit' you, bruh, so this is it, huh," Hawk said. "So what's the layout 'cause it has to be a precise and neatly laid out plan."

"Fa' sho', fa' sho'. Well, at first I was gonna hit the truck at CVS, right. Then I went and seen Chad and he was watching HLN, and they was talkin' 'bout these Sacklers brothers, the ones behind oxycontins, and shit," Maliss explained.

"Right, right," Hawk said.

"So then, I figured fuck that, that's another lick, you feel me, bruh," Maliss went on, as he guided the truck onto the interstate. Behind him, Lil' Wee-Wee eased on the interstate, careful to keep a safe distance.

"Fuck he goin'?" he thought, and pressed the gas. He remained as closely in tow as he could without being seen. As he followed them on 85 north, they headed out of Atlanta.

"I'ma kill these two dickheads first chance I get. I'm all in now, so it's whatever. Maybe this gonna be the whole shabang, ya dig," Maliss said.

"Right, right," Hawk replied nonchalantly.

"So I was gonna extort him, but why do that when we can make him come up off that receipt, or make him sign it over to us like they sold it. You know what it is," Maliss said.

"Yeah, I know that part, but how we gonna get around these dudes?" Hawk asked

"Oh, we gon' do what we do best, nigga. We gon' go get dressed, go up there to Lake Borton, look 'em up, and do some research. You know . . . find out 'bout their seminars or their guest appearances. We know they rarely seen, so we go hard or don't go."

"Right, right," Hawk agreed.

Ninety minutes later Maliss turned on to their mansion, off Nardella on Lake Burton. It had a seven bedroom, eight and a half bath, indoor swimming pool, a movie room, a game room, and a boat deck and water shed with a boat plane.

Lil' Wee-Wee kept going unnoticed. He punched the address in his GPS. "Damn, now this shit is too nice." He made a U-turn. "Fuck it. Now or never," he said, hyping himself up. He pulled up, jumped out, crouched low, and ran down the hill to the garage.

Let's get these bags in the crib," Maliss told Hawk. He walked to the back of the truck and . . .

"Freeze!" Lil' Wee-Wee yelled out the first thing that came to his head. Hawk swung around surprised, but Maliss swung into action. Grabbing his Draco, he fired off.

Lil' Wee-Wee got low and returned seven of his own. Maliss moved around the truck, trying to get a clear shot. More shots came as Lil' wee-Wee laid on the trigger. Maliss was pinned and Hawk was faced-down.

Lil' Wee-Wee suddenly gained a boost of the courage. "You gonna die today, fuck boy," He released several more shots.

Maliss shot again but still missed his target. When he came up from behind the truck, more bullets went whizzing past his head. He crashed into the trash cans and went down hard.

Lil' Wee-Wee ran to the truck and tried to pull the cover from it but it was too heavy. He kicked Hawk and he didn't move, as he lay motionless with blood pouring from around his head. Lil' Wee-Wee kept his Draco aimed and ready to fire as he rounded the front of the truck. Maliss was still covered in trash and trash cans and didn't appear to be moving.

"Told you, bitch ass nigga! Fuck nigga, I got yo' bitch nigga!" Lil' Wee-Wee ran to his Jeep and drove it inside the garage to transfer the goods back to his vehicle. He was little but strong for his size. Using the pure rush of adrenaline, he managed to get everything secured quickly. Hoping inside, he backed up fast. He smashed the gas causing the tires to squeal, en route to Hayneville with a Jeep full of dope.

"Hell yeah! I finally got that lame ass nigga. Bitch ass nigga. Now I gotta trick that bitch and I'll have her too, and whatever else he left behind. Can't wait to see how much work I got. Man, the city is mines," Lil' Wee- Wee shouted out loud. He turned up the music and rode the rest of way rapping along with his favorite song. *"Nigga you know we talk that stick talk / that stick talk / nigga you know we talk that lick talk, that lick talk!"*

165

Paper Boi Rari

CHAPTER 21

"Ahh Shit! I think my shit broke!" Maliss screamed, trying to sit up after being unconscious for 25 minutes. "Hawk, where you at, bruh! This shit crazy! A nigga done caught us slippin', boy. Yo, Hawk!" He sat up and shouted out for Hawk again. "Ahh, I think my chest bone is cracked or something. My shit on fire," he said, rubbing his chest.

He stripped the vest off to try to breathe better. "Hawk, good thing we invested in this military shit, huh, bruh? These shits are lifesavers, a nigga done cheated death again." He tried to laugh but it hurt too much. "Man, Hawk, what's up wit' you, you ain't sayin' shit, nigga." Finally, he made it to his feet and started to think Hawk was probably still knocked out from the shot. Slowly he rounded the truck and saw Hawk face-down in a dark pool of his own blood.

"What the— Aww, man . . . Hawk! Muthafucka! Oh my God, not my dawg, please Lord. . . . "

He rushed to Hawk's still body. "Come on, bruh, I'll get you to the emergency room, bruh, just hold tight, I got you," he said, pushing himself to move faster. But when he turned Hawk over he let out a cry no man should ever have to experience . . . "Nooo! No, no, no! Lord, why ..." He cried as he held his partner, his day-one, in his arms. He couldn't see Hawk's face because it had been blown off.

Lil' Wee-Wee had loaded explosive rounds into his Draco and a luckly shot had put a hole the size of a grapefruit in Hawk's head.

Maliss cried for his lost brother, tears he hadn't shed since his childhood. "Lord we done a lot of wrong, but I swear I never saw it ending like this." He said a silent prayer for his only brother.

After a few moments of grieving, he got up, cleaned the garage with disinfectants and left the scene. He took the GPS off his phone and called the police to report a shooting in the area of 355 Narnia, Lake Burton.

"I can't let you sit here, my nigga. They might take too long to find you," Maliss told the corpse.

The maids would only come in once a month to check on the residence, and he knew the law would contact him since it was his place, and he was Hawk's only next of kin.

"These bitches really wanna play wit' a nigga, huh?" he said aloud. He looked at his phone and saw multiple missed calls from Roe Black, Ayesha, and Lil' Rod. *Fuck, I gotta get a Lil' Rod with the work*, Maliss thought. He read Lil' Rod's text message:

R: Lil Fred DEAD bruh now 12 after me 5 questions, dont trip on the visit. I'll be n contact. Luv bruh.

"Damn, shit reversin' like a muthafucka 'round this bitch," he said aloud and pounded the steering wheel. He sent Lil' Rod a message back:

Bossman: Aight bruh. u gota catch me on da gram bruh. Changin #'s . . . b safe nigga.

Then he sent a text to Roe Black.

Ima hit u from new num, so when u c it you'll recognize its me, finna change #'s, something came up!

Bae: I'll be home real soon, bae.

After sending all the text messages, he threw the phone out the window on the interstate. "Lil' stupid nigga came to kill a nigga, huh? Didn't have a mask on like he 'bout that life, knowin' I'm really livin' like that. I got him, boy.

You shoulda finished the job, homes. They don't call me Maliss for nothin'. Now I'm 'bout to turn into psycho Maliss, watch this! Fuck nigga, I'm comin' to kill your whole family, boy . . . kids and all, pussy!

Ayesha stupid ass tryin' a nigga real hard too. Got my bruh killed with her hoe ass and shit! She gotta go too, fuck that! Nigga don't need no liabilities 'round, and a bitch you can't trust is a bitch back to dust!" he said to himself on the highway, heading back to his Atlanta home.

CHAPTER 22

Saturday, June 23, 2018
Ebenezer Baptist Church Atlanta

Maleek sat with his head on the pew in an all black suit by Giorgio Armani, wearing black Gucci loafers designed by Dapper Dan himself. He was mourning, trying to accept the reality that his best friend, his only brother, had exited earth forever. The pastor preached and gave his blessings to the deceased.

Ayesha sat quietly beside him, not knowing what to do to console her husband. He wouldn't let her touch him.

I wonder what his problem is, she thought, *he been stuck up and acting stank lately. Maybe he's havin' a hard time with Hawk being killed, but life goes on honey.* She looked at Maliss, as she continued contemplating. *Whatever it is, he better start showin' me some love and act like he see all this sexy fine woman, if he know like I know.* She sat up straight in her seat, wearing an all black blouse and mini-skirt with heels by Chanel—she knew she looked good. She turned her attention from Maliss and listened to the preacher give his sermon.

This ungrateful ass bitch got some nerve sittin' her funky ass in here actin' like so innocent and shit and got my dawg layin' in a casket. I can't believe I married this triflin' ass back-stabbin' ass hoe. On top of that, then gave her broke ass an extravagent life to be proud of, Maliss thought, holding back his rage. He then looked at his daughter Gabby with sadden eyes, thinking. *Look at my beautiful princess, she cryin' her eyes out about her uncle Hawk. She gonna take this hard, but it has to be done. A snake will always bite you no matter how good you treat it, it's just their nature.* Maliss sat quietly in deep thought, planning his next move.

The funeral was beautiful and everyone respected and loved the fine job Maleek had done to show respect to his brother.

Hawk was laid from head-to-toe in an all gold casket wearing an all white Balmain collar shirt with white Balmain trousers, a white Gucci belt with the gold buckle, and all white loafers by Gucci. The gold presidential Rolex and seven-carat diamond studs in his ears sparkled brilliantly, and the Steve Havrey tape-up made him look open-casket sharp. However, with the gunshot tearing away his face, those in attendance were only able to see a photo of him placed on top of the casket. Only Maliss and the coroner knew the truth.

"Daddy, why can't we see him?" Gabbie asked. This made Maliss tear up even more.

"Baby, he was shot in the face, so it's really nasty to look at."

"Oh, daddy, that's so sad." Gabbie squeezed his hand and started crying again. Seeing his daughter in such distress caused more tears to roll down Maliss' face, which made Ayehsa cry as well.

Maliss looked long and hard at the photo of Hawk, thinking, *Bruh, you know yo' big bruh need you, man. You left me like this . . . Man, we got memories, boy . . .* He laughed a little as his mind flash backed in time momentarily. *For real though, dawg, you already know I'ma handle the situation at hand with straight malice, partna!*

The more he thought about what had happened, the more his anger grew. He touched the casket, trying to control his rage. "Bruh, damn man . . . I just can't believe it ended like this, homes," he said to the photo of Hawk.

"I know you would want me to be happy, but I can't be, bruh. I'ma miss you, homes. I already miss you. That shoulda been my bullet, bruh."

Seeing her man so broken up made Ayesha burst into tears, and she hugged him tightly. He wanted to push her off of him but didn't want to embarrass them both. So he remained calm for the moment. When the service were over and everyone went their separate ways, Maliss stayed at Hawk's grave all night. He had missed forty calls from Ayesha and fifteen from Roe Black, even though he had big plans for both.

Paper Boi Rari

CHAPTER 23

Wednesday, June 27, 2018

This was the first time Maleek hadn't gotten up to eat breakfast with Gabbie before she went to school. Ayesha put Gabbie on the bus and kissed her goodbye.

"Is daddy gonna be alright, Momma?" Gabbie asked her mother.

"Yeah, baby, he will. He just need a little time to get well, sweet heart. Momma will see you later, okay?" Ayesha tickled Gabbie on her way on the school bus. Gabbie laughed.

"Okay, Momma. Love you." She kissed her mother and went to find a seat by the window, waving goodbye. Ayesha blew her a kiss and Gabbie caught it and placed it on her jaw. Ayesha smiled and shook her head as she walked back inside the house.

While in the kitchen, she fixed Maleek a big breakfast, hoping to get fucked to sleep after he had eaten a good meal. She fixed salmon patties, yellow grits, scrambled eggs with cheese, biscuits with a side of fruit cocktail, orange juice, and sat a warmed bottle of old fashioned maple syrup down on the platter, and carried everything upstairs. Maleek was still in the bed underneath the covers, devising the last touch of his plan.

"Baby, wake up, my king," Ayesha said as she rolled the breakfast to his side of the bed. "Baby, I fixed you a big healthy breakfast. Now get on up and eat, bae." Maleek didn't move. She reached under the covers and grabbed his dick to massage it but still didn't get the reaction she was hoping for. She lifted the covers and went in with her mouth open wide to give him the perfect wake up call.

Maliss couldn't reject good head. *I might as well,* he thought. Soon, his dick stood tall in her mouth as she deep-throated with the savage skills she was known for, until thick warm liquid slid down the sides of her lips. She swallowed all of him and kept sucking until she was satisfied he was empty.

"Good morning, baby," she said, after coming from underneath the covers, smiing

"Morning," Maliss said dryly. After all that work she'd just put on she was almost quick to catch an attitude, but she remained calm. "I fixed you a nice breakfast, bae.

Go ahead and enjoy it while it's still hot. Your daughter is very concerned about you. You never missed having breakfast with her before school," Ayesha said. 'I'ma go freshen up and when you finish I'ma put this good pussy on you and put you back to sleep, sir." She left the room and headed for the bathroom.

Maliss waited five minutes before getting up and pulling the bottom drawer of the dresser all the way out, grabbing the syringe. He quietly replaced the drawer and got back in bed.

He looked at the food on the cart. Being from the country he knew Ayesha knew how to throw down in the kitchen. He didn't really want it, but he also couldn't resist a good meal. Before he knew it, he had eaten everything on the plate, not realizing that he'd been that hungry.

He sat back in the bed, finally ready to put an end to this chapter of his life. He had already ensured the cameras around the house weren't recording. He knew the police would be coming to badger him with questions so he had prepared ahead of time.

Ayesha came out of the bathroom in powder-blue lingerie by Illegal Activity, wearing a pair of soft pink Christian Louboutin heels. The fragrance she wore was from Heat of Passion, also by Illegal Activity. Maliss' dick instantly grew solid. There was no denying she was a beautiful woman, one that he hated to have to delete. But her whorish ways and bad decisions had finally caught up with her. Her death was the bed she'd made for herself.

"This pussy is ready and extra juicy, bae. I want you to put me to sleep," she said in a sexy voice. *I'm definitely 'bout do that*, Maliss thought.

"Turn the camera on, bae," he told her, referring the to 90 inch screen in their room. "Put it on monitor. I wanna look at you while I put this big dick in your mouth, then see how juicy that pussy is while I'm deep stroking you slowly.

"Ohh, hell yeah, bae. I like the sounds of that," she said, rushing to set everything up. Once complete, she strutted back over to the king sized bed and stretched her hands far out, arching her back to make her ass sit up high.

She jiggled a bit and her ass clapped loud. Maliss walked behind her and stuck his face in her ass, eating her pussy from the back. Ayesha moaned in pleasure. "Ohhh, bae, just like that, that's how I love it," she said, making fuck-faces in the camera. "Lawd! Shit! Right there, bae, don't stop, eat this good pussy She wiggled her ass in his face, grinding her pussy on Maliss' tongue. "Ohh, fuck! I'mmm cummmin! Yes! Oh God, yes! Ummm ohhh, baby . . ." Maliss lapped it all up, every last part of it until the last drop.

Then, he proceeded to lick her wide ass. He pulled out a pair of Gucci hand cuffs and a Gucci scarf made by Illegal Activity. Stacking several pillows up high, he told her, "Lay on these, bae. I want that ass sittin' high when I drop this dick in you."

Ayesha shifted and stretched her arms out along the bed. He cuffed her to the bed posts, then got behind her and tied her feet to the opposite end.

"Sss, that's kinda tight, bae," she said.

"Shut the fuck up, stupid bitch!"

"Whhaaa, bae?" she said, confused.

Maliss made sure she was facing the TV screen for this part. "Dumb ass hoe, you done lost yo' mind!"

"Bae, what are you talkin' 'bout, you trippin'" she said, almost crying from fright.

"Nah, bitch, you the one trippin' 'round here. What you thought I wouldn't find out or somethin'? Bitch, you got Hawk killed with yo' whorish ass self!"

"No I didn't!" she yelled.

"See, let me tell you somethin', Ayesha, somethin' you didn't know. I had a camera put on your truck. Yo' truck was also bulletproof, that's why they didn't kill you. So I checked the camera to see who it was. And guess what, you stupid bitch? I know them muthafuckas. Stupid ass Dirt bag and Lil' Suwhoop from D-Block. So me and Hawk rocked them to sleep with a dirt nap." Maliss talked calmly as if he had all day. Ayesha listened with her limbs bound.

"Now, you remember the day you made 'Tanna walk from here?" Maliss asked. Ayesha didn't respond, so he continued.

"That same day we saw a black Impala ride by. You act like you ain't know who it was but you did. And that's why you can't be trusted. Then on top of that, you fake me out like you was goin' to see yo' fam, but went to fuck Lil' Wee-wee, not knowin' or carin' he was usin' yo' lame ass to get to me. You and 'Tanna both some ducks."

"Nah, baby, let me explai—" Ayesha tried to say.

"Fuck all that!" Maliss shouted. "You shoulda did that a long time ago. "Not only did this pussy get *my pussy*, but he made you turn on your own family. You put me and Gabbie in danger! Yous a dumb ditch!"

Instantly, Ayesha began crying, realizing what she had done.

"Yeah, save that shit. I used all mine for Hawk."

Maliss walked around the bed to look her in the face. "Now, this is the good part. The bitch-ass nigga had to be followin' me 'cause when I took Hawk to our stash spot all the way in South Carolina, this bitch ass nigga come out of nowhere, blastin' on us. Hawk got his head blown off and I took three to the chest. Luckily, I had a vest on. But the nigga robbed me for millions in drugs. And there you have it . . . the woman I married is a traitor, the mother of my child. So now the question is, where do we go from here," he asked, looking Ayesha in the eyes.

Ayesha was still crying and unable to talk. She was so scared. She knew she was defenseless, and she also knew what the outcome was going be.

Maliss began to walk around the room like as if he was giving a lecture in school. "Well, I can't lie, I'ma G, and I live by morals and principals, and I don't break them for no one, Ayesha. Today is yo' last day on earth."

Ayesha began struggling against her cuffs but it was worthless. Tears ran down her face from the desperation. Finally, she screamed.

"Bitch!" Maliss punched her hard in the ribs only to quiet her and not bruise her. She hollered again. He grabbed a pillow and placed it under her head, then pushed her head down into it, smothering her.

"See, Hawk woulda done the same for me. Real nigga shit," he said before he slapped her in the back of the head. "I might as well enjoy this pussy for the last time, huh?" he said, looking at her ass raised in the air.

"Maleek, no, bae, I'm sorry. I never meant for it to go like— Ahhh!" Ayesha screamed so loud it was heard throughout the house, but no one was there to hear it. Maliss had rammed his dick all the way in her asshole, down to this nuts and began grudge fucking her.

When her ass began to bleed, he snatched it out and rammed himself in her pussy. She cried for mercy but he ignored all her pleas and enjoyed the look on her face while watching the large monitor.

Maliss then stood over her and plunged a 20-inch dildo in her ass, using both hands for added force. The pain was so intense she passed out. He waved an ammonia stick under her nose and she shook awake with an asshole the size of a tangerine. She hollered blindly as he fucked her aggressively, cumming in her with pure satisfaction.

"Ohh, shit, I really needed that one. It's been a minute, huh?" He rose up off of her. "Aight, love, 'till death do us part, remember?" he asked, showing her the syringe. Ayesha pissed on herself instantly. "This here is uncut heroin, bae. You'll die a painful death, bitch, but don't worry, I'll take care of our daughter."

"Nooo! Please Maleek, please baby. Don't kill me. I know I fucked up, but don't kill me baby, please. I'm sorry, Maleek. I messed up! Maleek shot the syringe in between her toes, drew the needle back and pushed it back in, showing no emotion.

Quickly, Ayesha began to nod, her eyes rolled in the back of her head. She started shaking and foaming out of her mouth. Then with one last jerk of her body, she was gone forever.

Maliss cleaned up, untied her and made the scene look normal. Then he left to go to The Spot until it was time for Gabbie to get home from school.

CHAPTER 24

Maliss was on the internet doing some astronomical research on the Sacklers. "Okay, so Arther is dead, but Raymond and Mortimer are still around and they old as shit," he read as he waited for Roe Black to pull up. He checked the time on the computer. "The nigga should be here any minute. Gotta groom him on this shit since my dawg gone, damn!" he said out loud.

"So this is The Spot," Roe Black said when he walked in.

"Yeah, this is it," Maliss said as he got up to give him dap. "What it do?"

"Shit, chillin', what's good?"

"Shit, trying to put a few things in line to get back on my feet, a nigga took a major loss so I got to come back super hard, ya dig?" Maliss said.

"Yeah, bruh, I can dig it 'cause it's been very slow on my end too. I just been taking it one day at a time to make ends meet, you know. I ain't seen shit worth touching, so I been low key till I heard from you. Figured you might have something in the making," Roe Black said.

"This shit here gotta be precise, ain't no half-steppin', ya dig? I got a few things in the making, bruh. They very major, we could be *super* straight and it could last for the next twenty generations if it's planned right and followed to a tee." Maliss looked at him for a second before continuing to get a good read on him and to make sure what he was saying was soaking in thoroughly. "It'll be a three-step process. First, we have to hit a light lick, then the product has to be sold. Then, we'll take the profit and invest in ourselves so we can be able to pull off the last lick, ya dig?"

"I'm listening. So what's on the table as of now?" Roe Black asked.

"Aight, our first mission is to hit a cigarette truck."

"A cigarette truck? What you mean?" Roe Black questioned.

"I mean a Mac truck, nigga. We gonna clean the whole truck out, ya feel me?"

"Yeah, alright, so what's the plan so I can put my insight on it?"

"To move some shit that's big, you know . . . first we need another Mac truck, and that's where your expertise comes in at. After that come up, we map out a location to hit, catch 'em and take the trailor. Once we do that I already got a avenue to get rid of all of 'em for a whole sell price," Maliss said.

"Alright, so what's the price?" Roe Black said.

"I dig you, bruh, 'cause you ask questions. That's a good thing."

"Yeah, I just wanna make sure everything in order and balanced out, or added and subtracted from it. This is our life, bruh," Roe Black said.

"Now that's real, and that's why I admire yo' concerns, and I respect 'em. It's eight bands a box, the trailor should have at least five hundred boxes. You do the math."

"Damn, that's four M's," Roe Black said. "That's four M's!" he said again as it was processing in his head. "Hell yeah, boy. When you ready?"

"Whoa, slow down, young nigga. I'm on it. It'll be very soon. I'm studying the facts and what's not on it. Like you said, it has to be done right, this is our life. But I figure we hit North Carolina since we know they make cigarettes there in Winston Salem, ya feel me?" Maliss said.

"Fa' sho'. That makes sense to me, bruh."

"Aight, let me finish up the details on it then I'll relate them to you."

"Bet that!" Roe Black said excitedly.

"After we complete that, we gon' start our own pharmaceutical empire."

"Don't get me wrong, I need the money but selling dope take too much time for me, homes. That's why I resulted to the gun game," Roe Black said.

Maliss started laughing. "Nah, youngin', I'm talkin' legally, my nigga. We gonna manufacture oxycontins."

"Now how the hell we gonna do that?" Roe Black questioned again.

"Easy. We gonna make the ingredients to see what can be tweeked. If nothin' can't be tweeked, then we leave it as is, 'cause we'll have the proper documents saying we own the rights to the products, and that it is now rightfully ours to do as we please," Maliss said and leaned back in his chair smiling, knowing this would be the lick of a lifetime, one that he could retire on.

That was when Roe Black knew the man was a straight up master mind and that he had to be extra careful around him. Maliss was an abnormal nigga, nothing like he had ever seen before. He had to admire him. He was super smart, but at the same time, that's what made Roe Black fear him all the more.

This man has all these smarts, but he's just using them in all the wrong ways, Roe Black thought before saying, "So, how will we accomplish this matter?"

"I'm gonna give you a few pieces real fast, but I'm 'bout bounce. I have to pick up my little princess, bruh." Maliss then spoke a few details of his plan before locking up The Spot and heading home.

Paper Boi Rari

CHAPTER 25

Maliss had been under intense questioning for the last six hours. They were asking him the same questions over and over in different fashions until he was fed up.

"So what time did you leave, Mr. Davis?" the white detective asked.

"Man, you already asked me that shit," Maliss said.

"Just answer the fucking question," the big black detective said.

"Nigga, fuck you!" Maliss spat at him. In a flash the detective was in his face, almost with his huge hands around Maliss' neck.

"Now y'all just calm down," the white detective said, breaking up the commotion.

"Man, my wife is dead and y'all in this bitch actin' like I committed a crime or somethin'. Whether you finished or not, I'm through answerin' questions. I have to go console my daughter. So to you gentlemen have a nice evening," Maliss said and rose to leave.

"Hey, sir, we apologize but this here is just proper procedure," the white detective said, handing Maliss a card with his name and number on it.

Maliss dropped it on the floor and walked out. "Y'all know how to contact me if you need to."

"That arrogant son-of-a-bitch!" the black detective said. "I don't like that bitch nigga. Something's up with him, I can feel it."

"Leave 'em be, he's just upset right now, he'll come around. He may need us before we need him," detective Hobbs said.

Maliss walked into the lobby where Ayesha's whole family sat waiting for him with Gabbie. Ayesha's mother fell into Maliss' arms, crying, "Why . . . why, Maleek? What happened to my baby? She never even liked drugs. How can this be?" Mama D hollered.

"I don't know either, Ma. I never sensed it from her. Come on y'all, let's go home," Maliss said.

"It's because of you! You had her around all them drugs and she got curious, you stupid muthafucka," Mama D yelled and began swinging and hitting him. Maliss had to push her out of the police station before the cops messed around and stepped in, but they understood losses, and a mother's loss was unexplainable. She cried in his chest as he carried her to the car.

On the way home he explained to her that she was going to have to keep Gabbie for a while until he recovered from his lost. He told her he felt it was best since he wasn't in the proper state of mind to raise her the right way. Gabbie had cried herself to sleep in the back seat. She never knew the morning hug and kiss from her mother would be the last one, or the last time she would catch one of her kisses in the air and place it on her cheek.

Gabbie would be mentally scared forever behind her mother's loss, on top of the loss of her Uncle Hawk. Two losses in one week was enough to tarnish her at her young age forever.

CHAPTER 26

One month later . . .

Lil' Wee-Wee pulled up to his newly purchased $350,000 mini-mansion in Hayneville, Alabama. It was all Stucco with hardwood floors and marble all throughout. There were five bedrooms, six full bathrooms, and three half bathrooms. He had a swimming pool in the backyard with a gazebo, and it sat on a luxurious ten acres.

He hopped out of a McLaren 6755 Spider, ghost-white with charcoal black interior, sitting on 20 inch Forgies rims.

He wore a thousand gram Cuban link that had a one hundred thousand dollar charm, all 14 carat gold, Bottega Venta swim trunks that cost five hundred ninety dollars with Tom Ford slides that ran him another five ninety, with some Tom Ford shades, and a big-face watch on by Hubolt sports additions.

"What's up, bae?" he said, holding up a bag filled with super soaker water pistols and water balloons, showing Santanna. She stood in the door smiling with her two piece swim suit on by Valentino.

"Hey, bae," she responded. Lil' Wee-Wee had the money-walk bop going on. He was definitely feeling himself. It was dry in Montgonmery and in one month he had ran up two million dollars to the surrounding area with heroin alone. The Molly, ice, and spice were a plus that added to it. He had become a king overnight, with great success. He was fucking nothing but the baddest bitches the city had to offer and loving life to the fullest.

"Everybody will be here around four o'clock, bae," Santanna said.

"Well, we got some time to ourselves to hang out then," he said, looking at his watch, it was only a quarter till one. "Fix me a Patron with a splash of grapefruit juice, and meet me in the pool," he said.

Santanna smiled and strutted off to fix the drinks. She felt good living the high life, but nothing like Ayesha had been, but it was a start. Thinking of her deceased friend caused her eyes to water. She was sorry she hadn't gotten the chance to make things right between them.

"What you crying for? What's wrong?" Lil' Wee-wee asked.

"Oh shit!" Startled by Lil' Wee-Wee's presence she spilled the drinks everywhere. "Boy, you scared the shit outta me. Nothing's wrong, I was just having a moment, thinking about how our lives had gotten better. I'm so proud of you, baby." She leaned in for a kiss. Lil' Wee-Wee kissed her back, but was becoming suspicious of her, knowing how money always seemed to have that kind of negative effect on people.

If she helped me get to Maliss through her best friend, and fucked me behind her back, I gotta keep my good eye on her, he thought. "Yeah, bae, this is the good life. Now come on, let's get in the water. Where Mya at?" he asked.

"She's already in the pool," Santanna said. They all got in the pool, laughing and playing games. Lil' Wee-Wee had just done a front flip off the diving board, creating a huge splash as he belly flopped into the water. Santanna and Mya erupted in laughter.

"Aww," he said painfully, "that shit ain't funny." The laughter continued until the metallic sound of an automatic ratchet froze everthing.

"You get a four in a half for that. Come on, you wanna try it again? I'll wait," Maliss said, standing with his silenced Draco. "What's the surprised looked for? What, you thought you killed me? Well, here I am, alive and well, partna. But I'll give you this bit of advice, you should have."

Maliss looked around the spacious backyard, walking easily around the pool. "I see you doin' pretty well for yourself, homes. Yeah, this is a nice pad right here."

Lil' Wee Wee looked as if he was going to faint. Santanna didn't know what to think and Mya was just plain lost but knew her fun had come to a sudden stop. Nothing but the music from the stereo could be heard over the scattering of birds chirping.

"I'm disappointed. You mean you have nothin' to tell me," Maliss said. "After you killed my brother and tried to kill me, fucked my wife, tricked her to get to me. Oh yeah, I can't forget, then robbed me to come live like this, and now I'm here and you don't even offer me a drink? Yeah, I'm so disappointed." Maliss picked up Lil' Wee Wee's Patron and took a sip. He frowned and spit it out. "Still low-class nigga shit, I see."

Santanna was staring at Lil' Wee Wee in disgust. If he wasn't going to say anything, she would.

"Umm, Maleek, me and Mya don't have nothin' to do with this, so we I'ma just leave and let y'all figure it out," she said looking toward Mya who was floating on a water pad.

"Don't move! Sit yo' raggedy ass down somewhere, hoe! Maliss raised the gun at her and Santanna froze with fear.

"Where my shit at, homes?"

"That shit gone, nigga," Lil' Wee-Wee said. Maliss walked over to the radio by the pool that was plugged with an extention cord. He bent to turn the music up before taking a deep breath. Truthfully, he didn't want the drugs back anyway, they caused too much karma for him. "Where my bread at then?" he asked Lil' Wee-Wee.

"Look around you, homes. All that shit gone too. I went shopping. It's all gone, my nigga," Lil' Wee-Wee said.

"Well, now that's the wrong answer. Mya, I'm so sorry, baby girl. Gabbie will miss you."

Maliss kicked the radio in the pool. Sparks of electricity sizzled from the surface of the water as screams rose into the air. Just as fast as it began, it was over, and all three bodies floated soullessly.

Maliss left as quietly as he had come.

CHAPTERS 26

Lil' Rod was ducked off outside Richerson Lounge with his baby AR15 with the monkey nuts on it. He was high on Molly and he'd been awake for a few days. He couldn't sleep due to the stress from the local police looking for him, and he'd recently heard the Feds were involved.

He knew it was only a matter of time before it all ended for him. He was listening to his first cousin, 1st Degree, "Fuck the Law," on his iPad with his USB cord plugged in. He was proud of 1st Degree for making it out the mud. He had just watched him perform on the BET Awards. 1st Degree had made it to number one on the top 100 Billboard charts and had eight more singles in heavy rotation.

"You made it, cuz," Lil' Rod said out loud as he bobbed his head to the music, hitting his astronaut blunt of kush laced with spice. "You deserve it, my nigga. Stay down till you come up," he said to the song as if 1st Degree was right there. "I love you, my nigga. Rep that shit! Yah, yah, that way! We from da southside, that way!" he said. As the drugs started to take its effect, Lil' Rod thought, *this ol' bitch-ass nigga Red Dog put the folks on my line, pussy ass nigga, lame ass, snitchin' ass bitch. Probably was hoping the law got me before I found out.* Lil' Rod had an aunt that worked for the county in the sheriff's building who had told his mother that Ricky Davis had called the Crime Stoppers hotline and reported information that Lil' Rod had killed Lil' Fred, and that Rod was also responsible for pumping drugs into the city. This she was certain of because she was the operator for that day.

"Hatin' ass niggas in the fuckin' way. Nigga, get ya hustle up!" he yelled out. He rode in a black on black Z06 Vette with 40% tint on the windshield and 20% all the way around. It had

1200 horsepower to the rear wheel. He ordered it out of the N.O. from D.E.B. Auto Shop, a spot Maliss had turned him onto.

Picking up his phone Lil' Rod pulled up his Facebook page and sent Maliss an inbox message, then waited for his victim to come out of the club.

"What's up, Red Dog? You gonna beat this pussy up tonight or what?" Sherry asked, grinding her ass all on his dick.

"Hell yeah!" Red Dog said, squeezing her juicy phat ass.

Sherry was 43, caramel, five feet four, 150 lbs, with long kinky twist. Fine as hell for her age, she could pass for thirty-two.

"Hmm-huh, well we gonna see what your old ass can do tonight," she said tipsy.

J-Racks was being entertained by three 23-year-old fine college students. "Yeah, send more bottles of Nuvol over here for these young ladies. All y'all staying wit' me tonight, right?" he asked them.

"Yeah, daddy," they all said at the same time.

"That's right! Who's gettin' the dick first?"

The tall red-bone raised her hand and giggled, sucking her finger as if it was a dick

"Oh now, Red Dog!" J-Racks called out. He was ready, He had seen enough and got what he wanted.

"What's up, bruh?" Red Dog said.

"What's up, you ready or what, cuz? I'm good for tonight, nigga.

"Look at these hoes I got," J-Racks said.

"Yeah, shit, I'm ready too, for real-for real." They were both already buzzing pretty good and wanted to get into the main course of the night. Passing the bar J-Racks called out to the bartender, "On, Nard, put that on my tap, partna."

"I gottcha. Alright, bruh, you good," Nard said. J-Racks was the first out the door of the club.

"There they go right there! Bitch ass niggas," Lil' Rod said. He made sure his internal lights were off and left the car running. He slid out of the car, leaving his door cracked. Wearing a black hoodie, he walked slow with his head down, holding the AR-15 toward the ground.

"Come on y'all, we parked right over there," Red Dog said. J-Racks was playing pittie-pat on the girls' asses and everyone was enjoying the moment. If they would have been paying attention they would have seen the shadowy figure creep toward their way.

Lil' Rod crouched low and began jogging toward Red Dog. As he got closer he leveled his rifle at Red Dog's head. Red Dog was the first to hear the fast approaching footsteps but wasn't fast enough.

"Hey, partna, got a light?" Lil' Rod asked.

Red Dog looked back just in time to catch rounds from an automatic to his face. His head exploded like confetti. The girls screamed as J-Racks took cover, trying to pull his GLOCK out. *Blocka Blocka Blocka!*

J-Racks' body was thrown into a truck and he was dead before he touched the ground. His chest opened like a pork-n-bean can, and his still open eyes stared at nothing.

The three young beautiful women cried and plead for their lives. Lil' Rod smiled at their fear and aimed the weapon on them.

"Bang!" he yelled, then laughed. "Get the fuck outta here, bitches!" The girls took off as Lil' Rod ran toward his Vette.

People started pouring out of the club to see what the gunshots were all about.

All they heard was the Vettes tires spinning on the gravel as Lil' Rod spit loose rocks on them, sending the crowd running for cover. The Z06 sped all the way until it reached the streets. The tires found traction but with so much power in the engine it fishtailed loudly.

Police sirens were soon heard and getting closer. Lil' Rod tried to control the car but it was too much for him. It was also his first time driving it since he'd purchased it, so he'd had no idea how strong the vehicle really was.

"Come on, baby," Lil' Rod said to the car, "get right for daddy." He slid all over both lanes of the street out of control. The car spiraled wildly until it crashed its front-end into a fire hydrant and slid into a ditch. The police sirens were fast approaching, with Lil' Rod trapped in the wreck. He knew they would soon be right on him.

"Fuck that!" Lil' Rod grabbed his AR-15 and climbed out of the passenger side.

"Freeze! Get on the ground!" a cop ordered. Lil' Rod pulled the trigger, sending three wild shots to scare them off and give him time to flee.

A burst of multiple police weapons cracked off from their return fire. Lil' Rod was already on the ground running, then slowly stopped. Dropping his gun, he felt the three burning holes in his back.

"Damn," he whispered before he spat out blood. He knew his life was over. He had done too much to ask for anything else. He smiled at that.

Quickly a field of officers were upon him with weapons drawn. They showed no mercy and riddled Lil' Rod's already dead body with a shower of bullets. Everyone came into the streets to see what happened. Lieutentant Barns and Sergeant Hawkins made it to the scene and were the first to the body. Lt. Barns shook his head, recognizing Lil' Rod instantly.

"That's Rodrick Miles. The muthafucker's a coward, he would rather die than to face justice," Lt. Barns said, walking off to view the other two bodies.

"It has been a sad day for Phenix City, Alabama," reporter Melanie Rice said into the camera. "Three killed, two by the hands of Rodrick Miles before he committed an attempted murder on an officer who had no choice but to return fire. Miles died on the scene. It was believed that he had other charges pending against him as well. Lt. Barns is here to give us further details," she said, extending the mic to Barns.

"Yes, it is believed that Mr. Miles was a druglord here in Phenix City and the surrounding areas. He was also a person of interest by the FBI for a slew of other crimes including murder. It's sad he chose the easy way out instead of facing these accusations in a court of law. The other two victims were murdered by him, and they too were suspects that several authorities wanted for questioning for drug related charges. This may have been a drug war in itself but we are still investigating before we state them as facts," Barns said.

"Well, what about the police-involved shooting of the officer firing his weapon into Mr. Miles as he was fleeing, shooting him several times in the back? How will that be investigated," Melanie Rice asked.

"Well, yes and no," Barns commented. "Yes, if he was unarmed or no weapon was seen. Once shots are traded it is rendered self-defense. But the officer will be taken off duty and on leave with pay until the investigation is complete," Lt. Barns ended, and walked away.

"Thank you, Lieutentant Barns for that. This is Melanie Rice reporting live in Phenix City, Alabama for Channel 12 News. Back to you Sherry."

CHAPTER 27

Friday, July 13, 2018

Maliss was ready to pull out en route to Winston Salem, North Carolina to hit the lick, then to New York to sell the load. Though all day he had been having a funny feeling in his stomach, he brushed it off and charged it to the spicy food he'd eaten the night before. Then on top of that, Roe Black was late with the Mac truck which he should've had the previous day. Roe had just called to say he was on the way, so at least Maliss was relieved about that.

"Damn, come on, young boy, so we can hit the highway," Maliss said out loud as he looked at his watch, waiting patiently for Roe Black. He was just just about to text him again for the sixteenth time when he heard the diesel truck pulling up at The Spot.

Maliss walked out to the truck. "Damn, couldn't you have taken a little longer?" he asked with sarcasm. "I was on the final level of Angry Birds in there."

"My bad, bruh, but sometimes shit happens," Roe Black said dismissively.

Maliss hoped in the truck. "That's real," he said and gave the man dap before putting his seat belt on. Roe Black pulled into traffic and turned the music up.

I'ma be fresh as hell if the Feds watchin' / drop toppin' Z Head. Roe Black sang along with his favorite song as he glance in the mirrors.

"We should be there in four hours," Maliss said.

"Hey yeah, big bruh. I got the GPS locked and loaded. You can sit back and chill for now," Roe said, and Maliss did just that, going over all the negative events that had recently taken place.

***

This was one of the happiest days of Agent Malone's career. It was Friday, Friday the 13th to be exact, and one of the hottest months of the year. He had finally convinced his superiors to give him a warrant on the man he considered his worst enemy ever.

"I can't wait to see his face, Trish. He may just shit a gold egg behind this one," he said.

"What's up with you and this hard-on for this guy," Agent Patricia asked inquisitively.

"Well, my mother and wife both used to use oxycotins pain pills for their chronic pains, then our insurance stopped covering it, but by then they were addicted," he said as they waited at the Fulton County county line. "So, well . . . I did what the average person would do," he continued as his eyes began to glass over. "I went to the street dealers and started buying from them to keep my mom and wife happy because they were always complaining about their troubles and they encouraged me to do it. That's when I met Maleek!" he said with growing anger. "We did a few dealings and he had good affordable prices, so I would buy two bundles of heroin for $4,500. And that's a very good deal because they're really three thousand a piece."

"I see," Patricia said.

Malone was really crying hard at this point. "They both overdosed, Patricia! The shit had enough fentanyl in it to kill a thousand fuckin' horses, you hear me? The worst part of all this is I couldn't tell nobody that I had purchased the dope for them. So it's like I killed my wife and my mother, and you're the first person I ever told this to, Patricia," he said.

"Oh my God," Agent Patricia said. "Are you fuckin' serious?"

"Yes, I'm dead ass serious."

"Damn! That's like one of them Montana TV stories or some shit," she said. "I'm sorry for your losses, Malone. And now I see why you want this evil bastard so much."

"Yes. And today I'm going to send his ass straight to hell."

***

"After this, Roe my boy, you gonna be a millionare, my nigga. Overnight success, partna," Maliss said. "That shit gonna be light, though. Wait till we pull this oxycotin move off. Nigga, we gonna be Bill Gateing 'round this bitch!"

"Hell yeah," Black Roe agreed. "I'm gonna get me a yatch."

"Nigga, we gonna be sellin' yatchs! Fuck you talkin' 'bout," Maliss said enthusiatically. "The siminar will be in September, so we got time to set up the demo." He was about to continue when he noticed the police lights up ahead and the interstate road-block behind them. "What the fuck?" he questioned. "Alright, alright . . . just be cool. We good. Everything straight, right?" Maliss asked Roe Black.

"Yeah, bruh, we good. I got you," Roe Black replied, a little too imperturbably.

"Aight, we good then," Maliss repeated, in a failed attempt to make himself believe it was true.

They pulled up to the road-block thinking they would show license and registration and be on their way, but once the truck stopped, all hell broke loose.

"Freeze! Don't move! Get on the fuckin' ground with your hands up! Now!" Agent Malone had his gun aimed at Maliss.

Maliss slowly began reaching for his Draco because he refused to go down without a fight.

"Don't do it," Roe Black said, pointing his own weapon at Maliss.

"Man, what the fuck is you doing?" Maliss questioned. His expression showed his confusion, but at the same time, he had always listened to his gut.

Roe Black pulled his badge from underneath his hoodie. "You're under arrest. It's over, Maleek." Hearing Roe call him by his real name and reading the FBI Special Agent Smith name plate on the badge, he knew it was trully over.

Maliss smiled. "Fuck you!" He pulled the trigger . . .

"Oh now, chow time, bruh. Get yo' ass up, nigga," Hawk said. "Maliss . . . man, it's last call, bruh! You know you goin' to chow so let's go, nigga!" Hawk came in the cell and woke Maliss up for chow like he did every day.

"Wha- what the fuck?" Maliss said, waking from a deep sleep.

"Hawk, my nigga, you alive!" Maliss asked, both surprised and ecstatic.

"Hell yeah, I'm alive, fuck you talkin' 'bout, and I'm hungry too. So come on before they lock the door, bruh, or I'ma leave yo' ass. I ain't missin' breakfast, they got scramble eggs, biscuits, and gravey today," Hawk told him.

"Damn, bruh, I just had a fucked up ass nightmare. You ain't gonna believe this shit."

Maliss was now completely awake. He was in Talledega FCI Federal Prison with only three days remaining until his release. When they walked out of the cell Maliss saw Roe Black.

Roe Black was about to be released within the next ten days and they had plans of linking up when they got out.

Maliss had a few good licks he knew of. He looked at Roe Black on their way out of the unit, thinking . . . *Nah, it was just a dream, he wouldn't do no shit like that. That young nigga solid.* With that in mind, Maliss and Hawk went to chow.

To Be Continued...
Kingpin Dreams 2
Coming Soon

Submission Guideline

Submit the first three chapters of your completed manuscript to ldpsubmissions@gmail.com, subject line: Your book's title. The manuscript must be in a .doc file and sent as an attachment. Document should be in Times New Roman, double spaced and in size 12 font. Also, provide your synopsis and full contact information. If sending multiple submissions, they must each be in a separate email.

Have a story but no way to send it electronically? You can still submit to LDP/Ca$h Presents. Send in the first three chapters, written or typed, of your completed manuscript to:

LDP: Submissions Dept
Po Box 870494
Mesquite, Tx 75187

DO NOT send original manuscript. Must be a duplicate.

Provide your synopsis and a cover letter containing your full contact information.

Thanks for considering LDP and Ca$h Presents.

<u>Coming Soon from Lock Down Publications/Ca$h Presents</u>

BOW DOWN TO MY GANGSTA

By **Ca$h**

TORN BETWEEN TWO

By **Coffee**

BLOOD STAINS OF A SHOTTA **III**

By **Jamaica**

STEADY MOBBIN **III**

By **Marcellus Allen**

BLOOD OF A BOSS **VI**

SHADOWS OF THE GAME II

By **Askari**

LOYAL TO THE GAME **IV**

By **T.J. & Jelissa**

A DOPEBOY'S PRAYER **II**

By **Eddie "Wolf" Lee**

IF LOVING YOU IS WRONG... **III**

By **Jelissa**

TRUE SAVAGE **VII**

MIDNIGHT CARTEL

DOPE BOY MAGIC II

By **Chris Green**

BLAST FOR ME **III**

DUFFLE BAG CARTEL **IV**

HEARTLESS GOON **IV**

A SAVAGE DOPEBOY II

DRUG LORDS II

By **Ghost**

A HUSTLER'S DECEIT III

KILL ZONE **II**

BAE BELONGS TO ME III

SOUL OF A MONSTER III

By **Aryanna**

THE COST OF LOYALTY **III**

By **Kweli**

THE SAVAGE LIFE III

By **J-Blunt**

KING OF NEW YORK V

COKE KINGS IV

BORN HEARTLESS III

By **T.J. Edwards**

GORILLAZ IN THE BAY V

De'Kari

THE STREETS ARE CALLING II

Duquie Wilson

KINGPIN KILLAZ IV

STREET KINGS III

PAID IN BLOOD III

CARTEL KILLAZ IV

Hood Rich

SINS OF A HUSTLA II

ASAD

TRIGGADALE III

Elijah R. Freeman

KINGZ OF THE GAME V

Playa Ray

SLAUGHTER GANG IV

RUTHLESS HEART II

By Willie Slaughter

THE HEART OF A SAVAGE II

By Jibril Williams

FUK SHYT II

By Blakk Diamond

THE DOPEMAN'S BODYGAURD II

By Tranay Adams

TRAP GOD II

By Troublesome

YAYO II

A SHOOTER'S AMBITION II

By S. Allen

GHOST MOB

Stilloan Robinson

KINGPIN DREAMS II

By Paper Boi Rari

CREAM

By Yolanda Moore

SON OF A DOPE FIEND II

By Renta

FOREVER GANGSTA II

By Adrian Dulan

LOYALTY AIN'T PROMISED
By Keith Williams
THE PRICE YOU PAY FOR LOVE II
By Destiny Skai
THE LIFE OF A HOOD STAR
By Rashia Wilson
TOE TAGZ II
By Ah'Million

Available Now

RESTRAINING ORDER **I & II**
By **CA$H & Coffee**
LOVE KNOWS NO BOUNDARIES **I II & III**
By **Coffee**
RAISED AS A GOON I, II, III & IV
BRED BY THE SLUMS I, II, III
BLAST FOR ME I & II
ROTTEN TO THE CORE I II III
A BRONX TALE I, II, III
DUFFEL BAG CARTEL I II III
HEARTLESS GOON
A SAVAGE DOPEBOY
HEARTLESS GOON I II III
DRUG LORDS
By **Ghost**
LAY IT DOWN **I & II**

LAST OF A DYING BREED

BLOOD STAINS OF A SHOTTA I & II

By **Jamaica**

LOYAL TO THE GAME

LOYAL TO THE GAME II

LOYAL TO THE GAME III

LIFE OF SIN I, II III

By **TJ & Jelissa**

BLOODY COMMAS I & II

SKI MASK CARTEL I II & III

KING OF NEW YORK I II,III IV

RISE TO POWER I II III

COKE KINGS I II III

BORN HEARTLESS I II

By **T.J. Edwards**

IF LOVING HIM IS WRONG…I & II

LOVE ME EVEN WHEN IT HURTS I II III

By **Jelissa**

WHEN THE STREETS CLAP BACK I & II III

By **Jibril Williams**

A DISTINGUISHED THUG STOLE MY HEART I II & III

LOVE SHOULDN'T HURT I II III IV

RENEGADE BOYS I II III IV

By **Meesha**

A GANGSTER'S CODE I &, II III

A GANGSTER'S SYN I II III

THE SAVAGE LIFE I II

207

By J-Blunt

PUSH IT TO THE LIMIT

By **Bre' Hayes**

BLOOD OF A BOSS **I, II, III, IV, V**

SHADOWS OF THE GAME

By **Askari**

THE STREETS BLEED MURDER **I, II & III**

THE HEART OF A GANGSTA I II& III

By **Jerry Jackson**

CUM FOR ME

CUM FOR ME 2

CUM FOR ME 3

CUM FOR ME 4

CUM FOR ME 5

An **LDP Erotica Collaboration**

BRIDE OF A HUSTLA **I II & II**

THE FETTI GIRLS **I, II& III**

CORRUPTED BY A GANGSTA I, II III, IV

BLINDED BY HIS LOVE

THE PRICE YOU PAY FOR LOVE

By **Destiny Skai**

WHEN A GOOD GIRL GOES BAD

By **Adrienne**

THE COST OF LOYALTY I II

By Kweli

A GANGSTER'S REVENGE **I II III & IV**

THE BOSS MAN'S DAUGHTERS

Kingpin Dreams

THE BOSS MAN'S DAUGHTERS II

THE BOSSMAN'S DAUGHTERS III

THE BOSSMAN'S DAUGHTERS IV

THE BOSS MAN'S DAUGHTERS **V**

A SAVAGE LOVE **I & II**

BAE BELONGS TO ME I II

A HUSTLER'S DECEIT I, II, III

WHAT BAD BITCHES DO I, II, III

SOUL OF A MONSTER I II

KILL ZONE

By **Aryanna**

A KINGPIN'S AMBITON

A KINGPIN'S AMBITION **II**

I MURDER FOR THE DOUGH

By **Ambitious**

TRUE SAVAGE

TRUE SAVAGE II

TRUE SAVAGE **III**

TRUE SAVAGE **IV**

TRUE SAVAGE **V**

TRUE SAVAGE **VI**

DOPE BOY MAGIC

MIDNIGHT CARTEL

By **Chris Green**

A DOPEBOY'S PRAYER

By **Eddie "Wolf" Lee**

THE KING CARTEL **I, II & III**

By **Frank Gresham**

THESE NIGGAS AIN'T LOYAL **I, II & III**

By **Nikki Tee**

GANGSTA SHYT **I II &III**

By **CATO**

THE ULTIMATE BETRAYAL

By **Phoenix**

BOSS'N UP **I , II & III**

By **Royal Nicole**

I LOVE YOU TO DEATH

By Destiny J

I RIDE FOR MY HITTA

I STILL RIDE FOR MY HITTA

By **Misty Holt**

LOVE & CHASIN' PAPER

By **Qay Crockett**

TO DIE IN VAIN

SINS OF A HUSTLA

By **ASAD**

BROOKLYN HUSTLAZ

By **Boogsy Morina**

BROOKLYN ON LOCK I & II

By **Sonovia**

GANGSTA CITY

By **Teddy Duke**

A DRUG KING AND HIS DIAMOND I & II III

A DOPEMAN'S RICHES

HER MAN, MINE'S TOO I, II

CASH MONEY HO'S

By Nicole Goosby

TRAPHOUSE KING **I II & III**

KINGPIN KILLAZ I II III

STREET KINGS I II

PAID IN BLOOD **I II**

CARTEL KILLAZ I II III

By **Hood Rich**

LIPSTICK KILLAH **I, II, III**

CRIME OF PASSION I II & III

By **Mimi**

STEADY MOBBN' **I, II, III**

By **Marcellus Allen**

WHO SHOT YA **I, II, III**

SON OF A DOPE FIEND

Renta

GORILLAZ IN THE BAY **I II III IV**

DE'KARI

TRIGGADALE I II

Elijah R. Freeman

GOD BLESS THE TRAPPERS I, II, III

THESE SCANDALOUS STREETS I, II, III

FEAR MY GANGSTA I, II, III

THESE STREETS DON'T LOVE NOBODY I, II

BURY ME A G I, II, III, IV, V

A GANGSTA'S EMPIRE I, II, III, IV

THE DOPEMAN'S BODYGAURD

Tranay Adams

THE STREETS ARE CALLING

Duquie Wilson

MARRIED TO A BOSS... I II III

By Destiny Skai & Chris Green

KINGZ OF THE GAME I II III IV

Playa Ray

SLAUGHTER GANG I II III

RUTHLESS HEART

By Willie Slaughter

THE HEART OF A SAVAGE

By Jibril Williams

FUK SHYT

By Blakk Diamond

DON'T F#CK WITH MY HEART I II

By Linnea

ADDICTED TO THE DRAMA I II III

By Jamila

YAYO

A SHOOTER'S AMBITION

By S. Allen

TRAP GOD

By Troublesome

FOREVER GANGSTA

By Adrian Dulan

TOE TAGZ

By Ah'Million

KINGPIN DREAMS

By Paper Boi Rari

BOOKS BY LDP'S CEO, CA$H

TRUST IN NO MAN

TRUST IN NO MAN 2

TRUST IN NO MAN 3

BONDED BY BLOOD

SHORTY GOT A THUG

THUGS CRY

THUGS CRY 2

THUGS CRY 3

TRUST NO BITCH

TRUST NO BITCH 2

TRUST NO BITCH 3

TIL MY CASKET DROPS

RESTRAINING ORDER

RESTRAINING ORDER 2

IN LOVE WITH A CONVICT

Coming Soon

BONDED BY BLOOD 2

BOW DOWN TO MY GANGSTA

Kingpin Dreams

www.ingramcontent.com/pod-product-compliance
Lightning Source LLC
Chambersburg PA
CBHW070458260626
47161CB00004B/1362